The Cowboy Conspiracy

also by Larry D. Names

BOOMTOWN
BOSE
THE SHAMAN'S SECRET
THE LEGEND OF EAGLE CLAW
TWICE DEAD
THE CREAM CITY CONSPIRACY
THE HISTORY OF THE GREEN BAY PACKERS:
    The Lambeau Years—Part One
THE HISTORY OF THE CHICAGO CUBS:
    Whites to Colts to Cubs—1869–1900

The Cowboy Conspiracy

LARRY D. NAMES

DOUBLEDAY & COMPANY, INC.

GARDEN CITY, NEW YORK

1987

With the exception of actual historical persons,
all of the characters in this book
are fictitious, and any resemblance
to actual persons, living or dead,
is purely coincidental.

Library of Congress Cataloging-in-Publication Data

Names, Larry D.
The cowboy conspiracy.

I. Title.
PS3564.A545C6 1987   813'.54   86–32951
ISBN: 0-385-23233-0
First Edition

For Pat and Jerry,
With love.

The Cowboy Conspiracy

PROLOGUE

HAR-QUA-HALA. A Pima Indian word meaning "source of water."

Some white man got his directions mixed up and named a range of desert mountain the Harqua Halas. Around 1890, a lonely prospector found gold in those sunburned rocks, and a town was born. Danged-fool miners called it the very same thing: Harqua Hala. A semblance of civilization followed, and with the amenities of comfortable living came murder.

The town's more respectable citizens saw no reason to tax themselves simply to pay a regular full-time marshal, so they petitioned the Yuma County sheriff's office for a deputy to be stationed in Harqua Hala. Sheriff C. H. Farnsworth graciously granted their wish and sent Walt Phillips to man the new outpost of justice.

Phillips performed his duties in a likable fashion for nearly two decades. That's how most folks described Walt. Quite likable. Always seemed to be smiling. Even when he was arresting some drunken miner who was taking umbrage at having his evening of frolicking short-ended. With a Cheshire grin that was both warm and sympathetic, Walt bore all the verbal abuse heaped upon him by the miscreant. Those who knew Phillips used to say he didn't have an enemy in the world.

Then in early June 1912 someone put a load of double-ought in his belly late one hot, sultry night when he was making his regular rounds of the town, and the theory that Walt had nothing but friends was put to rest. Permanent.

Sheriff Farnsworth was so riled up by the bushwhacking of his lifelong friend that he made the long ride up from Yuma to investigate personally. After a week of hours and a month of questioning every man known to own a shotgun, Farnsworth was forced to admit that he knew as much when he left as when he arrived in Harqua Hala. No clues to the identity of the killer; no hints to what really happened; no one all that willing to talk; not much of a trail to follow; nothing to point him toward the villain.

Frustrated, disgusted, bewildered, and mad as a half-drunk Apache, the sheriff rode back to the county seat determined that the murderer of Walt Phillips would not go unpunished.

ONE

A knock at the front door interrupted Charlie Siringo's writing.

Annoyed by the distraction, he slapped the pen down on the oaken desk, then huffed a heavy breath of irritation. How could he work with so many interruptions? Grabbing the arms of the chair, he slid away from the rolltop and pushed himself erect as he could; deep into middle age, he could no longer straighten up to his full height of six feet. Before answering the midafternoon caller, he removed the ink-stained blue garter sleeves he wore to protect his white shirts when working on his tales of his active days in law enforcement, threw them down on the seat he had just vacated, then took down a black frock coat from the hat tree in the corner and slipped into it.

The silhouette cast on the frosted glass of the door was that of a short person. Messenger boy or delivery boy, thought Siringo, the deduction process a result of his nearly three decades of searching out clues while pursuing the likes of such desperadoes as Billy the Kid and Butch Cassidy. He reached for the door handle, turned it, and opened the door wide.

Messenger boy.

"Telegram for you, sir," said the lad dressed in a blue Western Union cap, collarless gray cotton shirt, black suspenders, brown knickers, brown-and-gray argyle socks, and brown oxfords that hadn't seen a coat of wax since leaving the mail-order house in Chicago. He held out the message for Siringo to take.

"Telegram, eh?" queried Siringo, almost in a grunt, as he eyed the envelope held shakily in front of him. He delved into a pocket and retrieved a nickel. Handing the Liberty-head five-cent piece to the youth with one hand and accepting the wire with the other, he said, "Thank you, Roger."

"Mr. Betterson said you might be wanting to send an answer off right away, Mr. Siringo."

Siringo cocked an eyebrow at Roger and said, "Oh, he did, did he?"

"Yes, sir, he did."

"Well, we'll just see about that."

Siringo split the seal on the envelope and removed the folded sheet inside. The paper crinkled as he spread it to read:

CHARLES SIRINGO
DALLAS, TEXAS
JULY 15, 1912

WALT PHILLIPS KILLED   STOP   BUSHWHACKER UNKNOWN
STOP   GOING   HUNTING   STOP   COME   ALONG   STOP
ANSWER   SOON   STOP

W. EARP
VIDAL, CALIFORNIA

Siringo rubbed his chin in contemplation and read the telegram again. The second perusal started his head bobbing and brought a curl to one corner of his mustachioed lip.

"Wait here, Roger," said Siringo. "I will be sending an immediate reply."

Siringo took long, youthful strides back to his desk. Without sitting down, he snatched a blank sheet of paper from a cubbyhole, picked up the pen with a flourish, dipped it into the inkwell, and wrote:

WYATT EARP
VIDAL, CALIFORNIA
JULY 16, 1912

SAD NEWS. COMING ALONG. WHEN? WHERE? REPLY DETAILS.

SIRINGO
DALLAS, TEXAS

After a quick proofread, Siringo blew once on the words to ensure the ink being dry, then folded the paper first in half, then in half again. Strutting like a much younger man, he returned to the front doorway.

"Get this off right away," he said, thrusting the message at the courier. "And, Roger," he added, digging into a vest pocket to get a coin, "here's four bits to make your feet move faster." He flipped the half-dollar into the air.

Roger snapped it out of midflight, displayed his delight with a broad grin, then tipped his hat. "Thank you, Mr. Siringo." And with that, he spun on a heel and broke into a full run.

Siringo remained standing in the doorway for a moment, watching the young man race down the street toward the telegraph office. As soon as the lad was out of sight, Siringo returned to his desk. He took up the pen again and addressed a letter to his publisher in New York. In short terms, he informed him that his new book about Billy the Kid would be delayed because he was off to live another chapter in his own life.

TWO

The Bucket of Blood Saloon on Railroad Street in Wickenburg was nearly void of patrons when Charlie Siringo closed one of its etched glass doors behind him. A solitary drinker stood at the bar that ran along the left wall of the saloon. In the back, a gent in a gold-pinstripe blue suit was keeping the faro dealer busy, and a third customer sat at the second of the dozen tables lining the right side of the hall; a quart of bourbon and two shot glasses waited patiently in front of him. The bartender and his charge glanced up at Siringo, but the gamblers ignored his entrance. The fifth man merely shifted his steely blue eyes in Siringo's direction, blinked, then trained them on the vacant chair next to him.

Siringo offered a nod at the fellow with his back to the outer wall of the building, then stepped over to join him. He stopped short of the chair and stared down at the man. A slight smile of recognition turned up the corners of his mouth. He took off his Stetson and plopped it down on the table. Then he seated himself.

"Long trip, Charlie?" inquired the would-be host softly.

"That it was, Wyatt," replied Siringo, also in a hushed tone. "Been here long?"

"Sat down only a moment ago. Haven't even had time to open the bottle yet." Earp reached for the container, uncorked it, and poured each of them a shot. "Hope you still like Kentucky Blend."

"Never drink anything else," said Siringo.

They raised their glasses in a toast.

"To Walt Phillips," said Earp solemnly.

"To Walt Phillips."

They downed the liquor, each in a single gulp. Siringo held out his glass for a refill and got his wish.

"That one settled the dust," said Siringo. "This one's for old times. Here's to Alaska, Wyatt."

"To Alaska."

They drank again.

The two former lawmen bore some physical similarities. Each was mustachioed, although Siringo's drooped a little further below the ends of his lips than Earp's did. Earp, the older, appeared younger; fewer lines in his face, the wrinkles also not quite so deep. Both men had short white sideburns and silvery-blond hair. Earp's leathery complexion was due to having spent more time in the desert sun and air in recent years; Siringo being just the opposite, having found more hours in his autumn years for inside pursuits such as his writing. When younger, the two men had been just the reverse; Earp was the indoors man, working mostly as a dealer and a bartender, while Siringo was riding the long road, chasing outlaws. Both men were very thin, almost to the point of being gaunt.

Earp scanned the room, then looked back at Siringo and said, "Pretty quiet around here, Charlie. I picked the right place to meet."

Siringo leaned back and added, "My thought exactly. This town wasn't nothing but a stagecoach stop when you and I were riding this country in the old days. All new folks here in Wickenburg. Shouldn't be a soul within a hundred miles what knows either of us now."

"Most everyone I knew back then is dead now. I've managed to outlive nearly all of them. All those boys from my Tombstone days."

"Masterson is still alive. Last I heard, he was living in New York City, working for some newspaper. Writes about prizefighters, I think."

"Bat always was a sport," said Earp. "That gambling blood of his and that hot temper is what got him thrown out of Denver, I hear."

"That's right," said Siringo with a smile. "I'm the one who told you that when we met up in Nome."

"That was a town, wasn't it, Charlie?" A faraway look glistened in Earp's gray eyes. "I've often thought about the raw towns I've been to in my life. Dodge, Wichita, Tombstone, Creede, Cripple Creek, Telluride, Nome, Goldfield, Tonopah."

"Tonopah, yes. I've never been there. What's it like, Wyatt? As rough as Tombstone?"

"Tombstone was a hard place, Charlie. The Clantons, McLowrys, Curly Bill, John Ringo . . . They all made it a hard place. Doc, Virgil, Morgan, and me . . . We made it a hard place, too. Looking back now, I wonder . . . if everyone didn't make Tombstone a hard place. If there was ever a place where a man could wake up any day of the week and find himself in a tight before noon, it was Tombstone. A man could be drinking and laughing, enjoying the good life one minute, and the next minute some young tough would be standing over his bleeding body watching him die. A man had to be ready to meet his Maker at any moment and just as ready to send some heeled stranger to the devil at the play of a crooked card.

"Tonopah as rough as Tombstone, Charlie? I'm too old to know. Too old to care. The difference, Charlie? Back then I dealt faro and carried a piece or two all the time. Now I prospect for gold with Sally and hope no one raises any Ol' Ned with us. That's the difference, Charlie. I've grown old."

Siringo lowered his eyes, sorry he had asked the question. Sorrier still that he had been reminded that both of them were well past half a century in age.

"Wyatt," said Siringo softly, "if you felt that way, why did you come on this . . . this hunting trip. I mean . . . Sally—"

"Sally tried to talk me out of it," interrupted Earp. "But when I explained to her why I had to come, she packed a bag for me. She's the best wife any man could ever wish for, Charlie. We spend weeks—months, sometimes—away from towns and other folks, and she never complains. I know it's hard on her, being out in the desert all the time, helping me look for gold and silver, and I try to keep her from getting lonely . . . you know, from missing other womenfolk. We do go to the Coast ever' so often, but we haven't been there in nearly a year now. So when this thing came up, I knew it would be even harder on her . . . being left alone in Vidal and all. But I told her I had to come."

"And what was it you told her, Wyatt?"

"Farnsworth," said Earp simply.

"Clyde Farnsworth?"

"The same. He's sheriff of Yuma County. Walt Phillips was his deputy. I didn't know Walt that well, but I do know Clyde. When I was running from Behan and that mob, Clyde took me and Doc through a pass that not too many men knew about back then and helped us get away fast."

"I always wondered how you and Doc got to Colorado so easily when Behan was after your tails. Farnsworth showed you the road, you say?"

"That's right, he did," said Earp, "and I promised him then that I'd return the favor someday. All he had to do was ask."

"So he asked?" Siringo inquired.

"He did."

"But why did you ask me to come along?"

"I recalled when we were up in Nome telling each other tall tales about days riding these parts and how you told me about the time Walt Phillips rode with you for a while when you were chasing Cassidy and Longbaugh. You told me how much you liked him, how Phillips always kept you laughing and helped you to keep going, no matter how rough it got. You said he was a friend, and to me, that meant you were willing to lay down your life for him.

"When I got Farnsworth's letter about Phillips being killed and he asked me to come to Arizona to help him latch on to the bushwhacker, I got to thinking about how this job needed a man who knows something about tracking down killers better than me, and you came to mind. And I thought of you sort of being in the same fix as me and how Phillips meant something to you. I figured you'd want to be along. For the chase at least, if not for the kill."

"You were so right," said Siringo. "I am somewhat in the same fix as you. Old. My best days behind me." He chuckled, then, as he scratched the back of his head, added, "You know what I've been doing, Wyatt? I've been writing books about my career with Pinkerton's. Pretty fanciful stuff, but . . . aw, hell, . . . it pays. Not much more an old lawman like me can do. When I got your telegram, it was a breath of fresh air. Put a bounce in my step, don't you know?"

"I do know, Charlie," said Earp with a smile. "That's exactly why I'm here. I haven't felt this good since I landed in Nome back in '99."

Siringo patted Earp on the shoulder and said, "Then it's settled. We're just a couple of old fools come together in the middle of the Arizona desert fixing to become a couple of dead old fools."

Earp snickered and said, "You've read the sign well, Charlie. That's exactly what we are."

"So how do we get on with it?"

THREE

Harqua Hala had five major thoroughfares and a lot of little alleys that the townspeople called streets.

Salome Road started out as a two-track marching straight as an arrow up the gentle slope of the desert floor to the foothills on the north side of the Harqua Hala Mountains. Then it wandered through the hills past Big Painted Rock until it switchbacked down the south slope to the usually quiet town of Harqua Hala. For a quarter of a mile, it paralleled a deep wash, running along its east side until the arroyo forced it to bend toward the rising sun and dead-end at the cleavage of a pair of rocky nobs known locally as the Bosoms.

Two streets junctioned with Salome Road.

The first, Gold Street, split off at the base of the foothills and ran at a thirty-degree angle to Salome Road for a quarter mile until it swung west along the foot of Gold Peak and through the mining district. It made one switchback up the peak and ended at the mines.

Harqua Hala's boot hill lay between Salome Road and the wash two hundred yards from where Gold Street split off. Cemetery Street started here and ran parallel to Gold Street until it ended at the mining district.

Main Street and Higgins Street, named after the town's oldest citizen and one of its earliest settlers, Lester T. Higgins, started at Gold Street, intersected with Cemetery Street, then looped together at the north base of the Bosoms.

The miners, for the most part, lived in a series of shacks—some of tin, others of wood—lining the west side of the wash. In a railroad town, the area would have been called the wrong side of the tracks. But Harqua Hala had no railroad, so the snobbish business people and the mining bosses referred to the area as Ditch Town. A half dozen painted houses fronted the so-called right side of the ditch along Salome Road.

The business section on Main Street was made up of six saloons, one bank, general store, livery, post office, barbershop, land office, stagecoach and freight office, druggist's with an ice-cream parlor, firehouse, boardinghouse, and jailhouse with quarters in the rear for the resident deputy sheriff. The newspaper building was around the corner from the jail on Cemetery Street, and a photographer's studio and a Chinese laundry were up the same street between Main and Higgins.

The mining district consisted of four buildings: smelter, foreman's shack, machine shop, and equipment shed. The office of the Harqua Hala Mining Company at the corner of Gold and Cemetery streets separated the two sections of the town.

Siringo and Earp were already familiar with the layout of the town, thanks to Sheriff Farnsworth, who had provided them with a map of Harqua Hala and his notes on the people who lived there. Siringo asked Earp if Farnsworth had made a list of suspects, and Earp, after first looking perplexed, replied that the sheriff was very much in the dark as to who might have shot Phillips. No clues, no guesses, no nothing. They were about to embark on a cold trail that had been dragged with brush, rained on, snowed on, then stampeded on by the phantom hooves of time. Siringo remarked, "I could say this is going to be like looking for a needle in a haystack, but I don't calculate our chances being that good."

Farnsworth did advise them, and both Siringo and Earp agreed, that their reputations might be a hindrance to their investigation. Therefore, traveling incognito became a necessity. Since both men had their initials engraved or stitched on many of their personal items, they chose names that would be compatible. Earp styled himself as Wade Eagan, a penny-ante gambler down on his luck. Siringo, with his Texas drawl, chose the name Clayton A. Stewart, a rancher looking to buy a spread near Salome and wanting to know what sort of immediate markets he might have for his beef.

The same as their meeting in Wickenburg, Earp rode into Harqua Hala first, arriving on the stage that connected the mining town with the railroad in Salome. Carrying a well-traveled carpetbag, he went directly to the Gold House, the three-story hotel on Gold Street where Main Street intersected with it. To accentuate the role he was playing, Earp's attire quietly bespoke his assumed identity: the seedy drifter. Black frock coat with frayed cuffs; powder-blue silk vest that had lost its sheen and was permanently stained around the pockets; charcoal-gray trousers that suffered from pilling and had been snagged on too many rough chairs; boots on which a dozen coats of wax couldn't revive a shine; and a felt low-crown that was sweat-stained around the band. Earp wore no tie or collar.

A dapper dude, wearing an eastern-type business suit, matching vest, silk tie, bowler—all in brown—and a white shirt with celluloid collar and appearing, by his clean-shaven face, to be in his late twenties, was in the midst of signing the registration book when Earp approached the hotel desk. The clerk, a balding fellow with a hook nose and auburn mustache that matched his eyes and typically dressed in a black suit, white shirt, and western tie, looked on with animated interest. He seemed pleased to have a gentleman as a guest at the hotel. Then he noticed Earp standing close by, and his entire demeanor changed. A dull frown drooped his face for an instant, then he shifted his attention back to the dude.

"I hope you enjoy your stay here at the Gold House, sir," said the clerk over the soft whirring of the ceiling fan. He was smiling again as he spun the registry around to read the signature of the new arrival. "I think you'll find your accommodations quite suitable to a man of your obvious good taste, Mr. Patton. I see here that you are an engineer by profession, sir. Mining, of course."

"No," said Mr. Patton. "Roads and bridges. You'll tell your boy to be careful with my surveying equipment when it arrives at the freight office. I can't lay out a good roadway if my equipment is damaged."

"Yes, sir," said the clerk. "I'll tell him to be extra careful with it." He banged the desk bell, and a uniformed bellhop appeared almost magically. "Take Mr. Patton's bag up to room six, Willard. Then report back to me immediately."

"Yes, sir," said Willard. The teenager grabbed Mr. Patton's leather suitcase and started toward the staircase.

Mr. Patton turned abruptly, and unaware that Earp was so close to him, he bumped into the former lawman.

"Pardon me, sir," said Mr. Patton, backing away in a start. "I didn't see you there."

"The fault is mine," said Earp. "I shouldn't have stood so close. I beg your pardon, sir."

"Think nothing of it, uh—"

"Eagan, sir," said Earp, offering his hand in courtesy. "Wade Eagan, late of Vidal, California."

"George Patton, at your service, Mr. Eagan." Patton accepted the friendly handshake.

"An honor to meet you, Mr. Patton."

Patton stared at Earp for a brief second, almost as if he were trying to make up his mind about whether he had seen this older man someplace before. "Pardon me, Mr. Eagan, but have we met prior to this moment?"

"I think not, Mr. Patton. A gentleman such as yourself would surely have made a lasting impression on a person such as I. Quite possibly I remind you of someone else."

"That must be it," said Patton.

"In another lifetime perhaps," joked Earp.

"Yes, perhaps," said Patton in dead earnest. "Still, I feel as if I have seen you before, Mr. Eagan. Or as you say, someone who resembles you quite distinctly. Whichever it is, I will recall it sooner or later."

"When you do," said Earp, "would you be so kind as to inform me who my look-alike might be? I shall be staying at this fine establishment for some time. Do you plan to stay here long?"

"As long as it takes me to do my job," said Patton.

"Then we shall have time to chat further, sir. I look forward to our meeting again."

"So do I," said Patton. "Now if you'll excuse me?"

"Certainly," said Earp with a nod. He watched the younger man turn and follow the bellhop up the stairs, a hundred-odd thoughts streaking through his mind at once. Then shrugging them off until a later time, he turned to the clerk. "I'd like a room, please, with a view of the street."

FOUR

After registering under his alias and checking into room number four, situated at the northwest corner of the hotel's second floor, chosen by Earp for its two-sided view of the town, the erstwhile gambler made the rounds of the local watering holes in search of one that would permit him to set up a game, whether faro, straight draw, stud, or blackjack.

The hotel owner forbade him the use of his bar, as did the owners of four of the saloons, each citing the new law in Arizona outlawing gambling. None of them seemed to mind that Arizona's new constitution also prohibited the sale of alcoholic spirits, a deal made in Washington for the granting of statehood, but one which the state legislature was at that moment repealing.

Earp was left with two choices by morning's end and opted for the Dutchman's, a two-story with a balcony over the front boardwalk and a stairway up the back for customers who wished to practice some semblance of social discretion after patronizing the ladies-in-residence upstairs.

Big George Kramer owned and ran the Dutchman's. The more educated would have described him as fitting the part of Shakespeare's Falstaff. Tall of height, robust of girth, silvery handlebar mustaches well curled, black-streaked gray hair perfectly parted down the middle of his huge pate and held in place with an extra daily dash of brilliantine, sleeves rolled halfway up massive forearms, bull neck, onyx eyes, yet rosy-cheeked, and a gold grin that was the result of being smashed in the mouth with the mean end of a bung starter. Kramer dealt with Earp with all the pugnacity of a bulldoggish banker.

"From the looks of you," said Kramer during the negotiations, "you are no cheat. So I will not have to warn you about what I do to crooked tinhorns." Eyeing Earp's sides, Big George added, "Lift your arms. I want to search you for weapons."

Earp complied, saying, "There was a day when I would have given argument, Mr. Kramer, but—"

"But those days are long gone," interrupted Kramer. He made the search and came up with nothing. "Just as I thought. You've lived too long to be stupid. Okay, old-timer, you can have your game here. You buy your own whiskey. I don't give away my stock to no one. I assume you don't have any of your own gear, but not to worry. I have ample supplies of fresh playing cards and my own custom-made chips. All denominations. I'll set you up each day as the house, then when you cash in at the end of the night, you pay for any losses and I'll take twenty percent of your winnings for the rent of my table."

"Stiff terms, Mr. Kramer," said Earp. "I was thinking more along the lines of five percent."

"Fifteen percent, then."

"Make it ten, and I'll see to it that my clients never have an empty glass."

"Done," said Kramer, extending his giant's hand to seal the bargain.

"I will begin play tonight," said Earp, returning the grip. "After I've eaten."

Earp returned to the Gold House in time to see Siringo climb down from the chestnut gelding he had purchased in Salome. They made eye contact but only for an instant, neither wishing to reveal to anyone who might be looking on that they were the least bit acquainted with each other. Earp entered the hotel, while Siringo tied up his mount and removed his saddlebags from the animal's back. As Siringo entered the lobby, Earp stepped through the doorway of the restaurant.

The room was sparsely furnished but not without a touch of Victorian elegance. A molded white ceiling overlooked the papered walls, the pattern of which was vertical stripes and lines— one gray with an olive green to each side forming a tricolor of sorts and each threesome separated by a yellow ocher line. Each table was covered with a yellow cloth. The settings consisted of pattern-less pewter knife, fork, and spoon, placed in the proper order to left and right of a red cloth napkin. Thirsty, sickly ferns grew out of Mexican clayware pots in each of the room's corners. Two ceiling fans swished the air in the vain attempt to beat off the dry desert heat. Three gaslights on opposite walls and a pair of long windows through which diners could view the street provided the illumination.

Only one other customer, George Patton, the road engineer, was present, which was understandable considering the time of day: midafternoon. A middle-aged woman with thin reddish-and-gray hair tied back in a bun and wearing a white apron over a dark brown dress waited beside Patton's table, prepared to take his order. Patton glanced up from the menu in his hands to see Earp, smiled politely, then stood up.

"Mr. Eagan, will you join me?" asked Patton.

"Thank you, sir," said Earp. "I will." He moved to the square table and took the chair to Patton's right, placing himself in a position where he could observe all three of the room's entrances at once.

"Coffee, mister?" asked the waitress, as she offered Earp a menu.

"Black, no sugar," replied Earp. He glanced at the menu but didn't accept it. "Just bring me a beefsteak. Rare. And a couple of slices of Texas toast. Light on the butter."

"Would you care for a vegetable with your steak?"

"I suppose you wouldn't have any fresh peas, would you?"

"They come out of a can around here, mister," the waitress said tersely. "We got raw-fried potatoes, if you're of a mind to have them."

"No, thank you. I'll do without the vegetable. The steak and toast will do."

"And you, sir?" asked the waitress, addressing Patton. "What will you have?"

"I'll have the same as Mr. Eagan here," said Patton, "and you can add the potatoes to my plate."

"Very good, sir."

Before she could depart for the kitchen, a third man, wearing wooden-heeled Mexican boots, tan suit with no vest, black string tie, brown high-collar shirt, and brown Stetson, entered the dining room and approached Patton and Earp's table. His coat was open and pulled back on the right side, exposing a Colt .44 Peacemaker in a black leather holster on his hip. There was a mean look to his dark eyes that was accented by pockmarked cheeks and a wisp of a black mustache that tried desperately to distract an onlooker from an ugly scar that ran down the left side of his nose to his upper lip, interrupted only by the nostril on the same side of his face. The waitress took instant note of him, and the expression on her face said she wasn't pleased by his presence.

"Bring an extra cup of coffee, Emma," said the newcomer. He dropped a glare on Earp, ignoring Patton completely, then seated himself in the chair opposite the older man.

"I don't believe you were invited to join us," said Earp, a suspicious eye on the youthful intruder.

With his left hand, the newcomer pulled back the lapel of his coat to display a deputy sheriff's badge pinned to the pocket of his shirt. Looking Earp squarely in the eye, he said, "This is all the invite I need, gambling man."

Earp surprised himself by coldly saying, "That piece of tin gives you no cause to be rude." No sooner had he said the words, he began to wonder how many times he had behaved in the same manner when he was upholding the law. Another sign of age, he thought.

"Call it what you will, gambling man," said the deputy. "I'm here to ask you some questions, and I ain't leaving till I get some answers."

"I'll get the coffee," said Emma, suddenly visibly distressed. She scurried off for the kitchen but glanced back over her shoulder just before pushing through the swinging door.

"Mr. Eagan is right," said Patton. "Your authority as an officer of the law does not give you the right to annoy peaceable citizens."

"I apologize to you, sir, for disturbing your meal," said the deputy, "but this man is a gambler, and gambling is against the law in Arizona."

"Even so—"

"Please, Mr. Patton," interrupted Earp, holding up a hand to stay any further interference from the dude, "I can handle this affair."

"Is that so?" snarled the deputy.

"Yes, it is so," said Earp. "You might start off by introducing yourself properly, and taking a friendlier tone with me just might make me more cooperative."

"Do tell, old-timer. Hell, you're just like all the old geezers I've ever met around here. You all think you're hard 'cause you're from the old days. Well, you just listen, old-timer. Your day is long gone, and now it's my turn. So shut up and start answering my questions."

"Your name first," said Earp adamantly, his voice suddenly fired by the forge of years of dealing with young whelps with chips on their shoulders that were too heavy for their weak spines.

"I don't believe you heard me, old-timer," growled the deputy as he grabbed Earp's right wrist with his left hand and reached for his Peacemaker with the other.

Earp got another surprise from himself. The instincts that had seen him through many a skirmish in his younger days suddenly resurfaced. Quite aware of not being heeled, Earp reversed the deputy's hold in one motion, slid away from the table in another, then jerked the insolent lawman across the vacant chair in a third. The quick counterstroke caught the deputy off guard. As he sprawled over the seat of the straight-back, he dropped his Colt to the floor and his kicking feet knocked over his own chair and bumped the table, rattling the flatware. Earp gave another pull, and the impudent knave crashed face down at Earp's feet. In one more heartbeat, Earp had his right boot firmly planted on the back and side of the deputy's neck, pinning him to the wood.

Patton jumped to his feet, shoved his right hand inside his coat, but hesitated to interfere, feeling positive that the older man was in total charge of the situation. He withdrew his hand but remained aloof, prepared to step in if needed.

"Now about your manners, Deputy," said Earp.

"The hell, you say!" the deputy grunted.

"Mr. Patton," said Earp without turning to look at the man he was addressing, "what we have here is a lack of respect. It seems that the younger generations still haven't learned to respect their elders." Then he added, "Present company excluded, of course."

"You go to hell!" the prostrate man swore.

"Deputy," said Earp through gritted teeth, while pressing his foot down harder, "do you realize how close you are to meeting your Maker? With one quick stomp of my heel, I could snap that scrawny neck of yours. Ever see a man with a broke neck?" He didn't wait for an answer and proceeded to describe an imaginary victim of such an incident. "He kicks for a little bit, then dirties all over himself because he's lost control of everything from the neck down. And if he's lucky, he dies in a few seconds. If he's not, he suffers something awful those last few minutes of life." Earp paused to let that sink into the deputy's brain. "But maybe it might not break. Maybe I'll only crush your windpipe. Then you'd just choke to death. Take maybe five minutes or so. Ever choke on a piece of tough beefsteak, Deputy? I'll bet you have. Not too pleasant a feeling, is it? Not being able to breathe. No, it's not pleasant at all." Earp applied one more ounce of pressure and added, "Now I'm going to ease up a bit, Deputy, and I only want to hear one thing from your mouth. Your name."

"Deputy Sheriff Jacob Poole," the lawman croaked.

"Well, Deputy Poole," said Earp, "if you promise not to abuse that authority you so readily brandished a moment ago, I will let you rise, and we will start this conversation anew. Are you agreed?"

"Yes, sir."

Earp removed his foot, and Poole rolled over on his back. The older man held out a hand, and the younger man warily accepted the assistance to his feet. Earp held the grip firmly for a few extra seconds, letting the deputy know that he had the strength to lay him flat again if need be.

"Deputy Poole," said Earp congenially, "I am Mr. Wade Eagan, late of Vidal, California." He released Poole's hand. "And this is Mr. George Patton. Mr. Patton is a road engineer, and as you already know, I am a gambler by trade. This very day I have consummated a business transaction with Mr. George Kramer of the Dutchman's." Earp waved toward the table. "Mr. Patton and I were about to eat dinner, Deputy Poole. Would you care to join us?"

While rubbing his neck where Earp's boot had been, Poole peeked out of a corner of an eye and spotted the Peacemaker on the floor beside Patton's foot. The deputy's shift of view didn't go unnoticed by Earp, who calmly stooped and picked up the revolver for him.

"I believe this is yours, Deputy," said Earp, offering the weapon to Poole butt first.

Poole took the gun, a sheepish blush to his cheeks, and said, stammering, "Thank you, Mr. Eagan." He holstered the Colt but remained standing.

Emma returned from the kitchen, carrying three white ceramic cups and a tin pot of coffee. Nervously, she put the cups on the table, then waited for the men to make up their minds about if and when they would be sitting.

"Please, Deputy Poole," said Earp, again motioning for the lawman to join them at the table. Earp sat down and insisted for a third time. "We have a new start, so let's not spoil it now."

"Gambling," Poole stuttered, "is against the law . . . here . . . in Arizona."

"I am assured by Mr. Kramer," said Earp, "that this is only a temporary miscarriage of justice, the same as the prohibition against the consumption of alcoholic spirits. Are you telling me Mr. Kramer has led me astray in this matter?"

Poole didn't know what to answer. Big George Kramer held sway in Harqua Hala over more than the Dutchman's, and few dared go against him.

"No," said Poole finally, "he didn't tell you wrong."

Earp offered a confident smile and said, "Then we have a mutual understanding?"

"Yes, sir," said Poole.

"Good! Now that we've settled that matter, why not join us?"

Poole seated himself, and Emma poured the coffee.

Patton still stood, transfixed, unable to utter a sound, for it suddenly struck him that Mr. Wade Eagan bore a striking resemblance to a picture—actually, a newspaper lithograph—of Wyatt Earp he had once seen in a New York City newspaper. And how odd, he thought, their initials were the same, too. A mere coincidence? Or—? Or what? A charade of some sort?

With the presence of Deputy Poole, this was neither the time nor the place to be inquiring of Mr. Eagan. A later, more discreet moment would be proper. After all, maybe Mr. Wade Eagan—or Wyatt Earp, if that was who he really was—had as much to disguise as he did.

FIVE

Horace Beal was the editor and publisher of the Harqua Hala
Miner. He was alone, busily writing at his desk, when Charlie
Siringo entered the business office of the newspaper.

"May I help you, sir?" Beal asked, looking up from his work. He
wore a visor to protect his eyes from the glare of two kerosene
lamps on his desk, and ink-stained red garter sleeves covered his
forearms. From the way he squinted, it was obvious that a pair of
spectacles would be well worth the price, but he had none.

"Yes, sir, you may help me," said Siringo. "I'm looking for the
proprietor of this fine establishment."

A smile crooked its way across Beal's razor-thin lips, and he
immediately popped to his feet, rising to a height that was somewhat less than that of the average man. With short, controlled
steps, he went to greet the visitor; in Beal's mind a potential
advertiser at best, subscriber at least.

"I am he, sir. Horace Beal, at your service." He extended a small
hand, which was in turn engulfed by Siringo's.

"Clayton A. Stewart is my name, Mr. Beal." He released the
editor's grip. "Late of Dallas, Texas."

"You are a long way from home, Mr. Stewart. Am I to understand that you are seeking greener pastures?"

Siringo smiled and waved a friendly finger in the air, saying,
"Ah, you astound me, sir. You truly are a man of letters, and may I
add, maybe even gifted with clairvoyancy?"

"Clairvoyancy, Mr. Stewart?"

"Why, yes, sir. Clairvoyancy. You mentioned 'greener pastures.'
That is the precise purpose of my visit. I am in the market for land,
sir. An acreage for a cattle ranch, if you will. And you, sir, recognized that fact immediately, and thus the reason for my observation that you may be gifted with clairvoyancy."

Beal smiled and nodded his understanding. "Yes, now I realize what you meant, Mr. Stewart. Yes, I can see why you might think me clairvoyant. But I assure you, sir, that is one thing I am not."

"But," said Siringo, "you are the publisher of this newspaper, are you not?"

"Yes, sir, I am that."

"Then you may perform a service for me, Mr. Beal."

Beal appeared puzzled and asked, "A service, Mr. Stewart? I am no land agent."

"No, sir, I expect you are not. However, I should think that in your position as publisher you would be the most knowledgeable man in these parts. Am I not correct in that assumption, sir?"

Beal loved the flattery but made a feeble attempt at modesty just the same. "You honor me, Mr. Stewart. If information is what you seek, then you have come to the right place. There is no other who knows as much about this locality as I."

"Exactly my suspicion, Mr. Beal."

"Well, sir, then how may I help you in your search for 'greener pastures'?"

Siringo stuck his thumbs into his vest pockets and threw back his shoulders. "I believe I have already found the land, Mr. Beal, although not all of it. In the valley, near Salome."

"Near Salome, you say?"

"Yes. To the west and north of the town. There are three sections available, but I am desirous of five. The two additional sections I covet seem to be tied up by some mineral-rights dispute and some outfit called the Triple H Land Company. Or so I was told by the land agent in Yuma in a letter I received from him only yesterday."

Siringo reached inside his coat and produced the letter, all properly addressed to his alias in Salome and from G. Whitmer, a land agent in Yuma. He took the letter from its envelope and presented it to Beal for his perusal. Beal read the missive quickly, then returned it to Siringo.

"As you can see by Mr. Whitmer's reply to my inquiry," said Siringo, "the sections I wish are unavailable, and he can shed no light on the mineral-claims dispute or who owns the Triple H Land Company. He does mention, however, that the Triple H Land Company has an address in Phoenix. I have written to them concerning the section under their control, but I don't expect a reply for several days. In the meantime, I thought I could make some inquiries here in Harqua Hala, and you seemed to be the logical starting place."

Beal had listened intently to Siringo, nodding at the end of each sentence and occasionally rubbing his chin as if he were studying on the problem.

"I have a plat map of the area, Mr. Stewart, but I don't recall ever having seen the name of the Triple A Land—"

"Triple H," Siringo interrupted, correcting Beal's error.

"Yes, Triple H. As I was saying, I don't ever recall seeing the name on my map. And as for mineral-rights disputes, I was unaware that any claims had ever been staked in the valley."

"They aren't in the valley, Mr. Beal," said Siringo. "The land in question is only partially in the valley. A good third of it consists of the eastern foothills of the Brenda Mountains. The only map I've seen of the area does not show the owners of these claims. Perhaps your map does."

"Yes, I believe it does. Would you care to look at it?"

"A capital idea, Mr. Beal."

Beal walked away from the counter toward the rear of the room and passed through a doorway. In a moment, he reemerged with a long paper tube with a shoestring tied around it. He placed the cylinder in front of Siringo, untied the bow, pocketed the string, then spread the map on the countertop.

"We are here," said Beal, pointing a finger at a little square that designated Harqua Hala, "and this is Salome. Now, you say the five sections you are interested in are located north and east of Salome." He moved his digit toward Wickenburg.

"No, I said north and west of Salome," said Siringo, correcting Beal a second time.

"Yes, of course, you did." He reversed direction with his finger and went to the proper area. "You mean these two sections marked as government land and this one belonging to the railroad? These are the three sections you say are available to you now?"

"That's correct," said Siringo. It was his turn to point to places on the map. "I am certain the Southern Pacific will sell me six hundred and forty acres of their section bordering the tracks and lease the remainder of the section to me, and I have no doubt that a government lease is available for the other two sections. It's this section owned by the Triple H Land Company and this one with the mining claims that I am having difficulty with. As you can see, the foothills of that region are literally peppered with mining claims. I see that many of them are owned by the Harqua Hala Mining Company. I will have to talk to them about leasing grazing rights to me, but if I am to graze my cattle on their land, I will also have to lease the rights from the other claimants as well."

"Do you really think you can graze cattle in that desert, Mr. Stewart?"

"Desert now, Mr. Beal, but with a little water and some good seed, it'll bloom to a literal Garden of Eden. Reclamation, Mr. Beal. That's the ticket to the future of the desert. Mr. Roosevelt recognized that fact, and now they are soon to complete construction on the first great dam of the West. Soon they will be harnessing raging rivers throughout this vast wasteland, and then the West will be as green as the East and twice as productive. Mark my words, Mr. Beal. Mr. Roosevelt has performed a great service for this proud land of ours by pushing through the Reclamation Act."

"If that was all he'd done," Beal mumbled.

"Pardon, Mr. Beal?"

"I said, or started to say, even if that was all he'd done, then he would still be remembered as a great President."

"That he would, Mr. Beal. That he would. But from what I read in the newspapers, Mr. Roosevelt is of the mind that he has not finished his task as leader of this great nation. Talk is he plans to make a third-party effort in the forthcoming campaign."

"The Progressives are behind him a hundred percent, Mr. Stewart. The dispatches I've been receiving say they'll be meeting early next month to formally nominate Mr. Roosevelt as their candidate for the presidency. I can't see the good of it. As much as I admire the man, I can't believe he has any chance of winning the election. The Republican bosses are saying the only thing he'll accomplish will be to make Wilson the next President of the United States. And you know what that will mean to this country? Tammany Hall and the eastern bosses running the country again. What this country needs now is a Westerner in the White House. A Progressive—"

"Pardon my interruption, Mr. Beal," said Siringo, politely trying to hide his annoyance and boredom, "but I've always made it a policy not to discuss politics or religion. Both subjects tend to make more enemies than friends."

"Forgive me, sir," said Beal. "I was getting a little carried away."

"Not at all, sir, but perhaps you should save that zeal for the editorial page, where it could do its best work."

"Quite right, Mr. Stewart. Quite right."

"As I was saying," said Siringo, returning to the subject of his visit, "I believe I have found the land I need, but I don't know about markets. Markets in these parts, I mean. Of course, there is the railroad in Salome that could take my cattle elsewhere, but I'm more interested in immediate markets. Like here in Harqua Hala."

"I see. Precisely what information would you like to know?"

"Precisely this. How healthy is the economy of this community?"

"The mines, you mean? How long will the gold hold out? Well, sir, the mining company has said there is enough gold in these mountains to last the century."

"The century, you say?"

"The century, sir. Harqua Hala is here to stay."

"I am impressed by that fact but still troubled by another. While in Salome, I heard that this is a rowdy place. So rowdy that the recent murder of a peace officer of good repute has gone unpunished. Is this true, Mr. Beal?"

"That much is true, sir. Early last month our deputy was shot down late one night while making his rounds of the town, and yes, the killer has not yet been found out." Beal looked over his shoulder for an instant, then added, "I can find a copy of the number where I printed the story of the crime, if you wish to know all the particulars. Of course, there weren't many details. He was shot with—"

"No, thank you, sir, that will be unnecessary. Your word on the matter is sufficient."

"Well, all right, but I can assure you, Mr. Stewart, that Harqua Hala is not a rowdy place. No more so than any other mining community."

"Well, I will have a firsthand look for myself over the next several days. I will be staying at the Gold House until I've cleared up all the business concerning the land leases. Speaking of which, may I copy the names of the claimants from your plat map?" Siringo stuck a hand inside his coat and said, "I have my own pencil and a notebook."

"Certainly, Mr. Stewart. Help yourself. I have work to do, so if you will excuse me?"

"Thank you, Mr. Beal."

Siringo went about carrying out the masquerade to the fullest degree, but before he could inscribe in his notebook a fraction of the names on the map, he was distracted by the office door opening. Two men entered. Siringo summed them up with a trained eye.

The older of them appeared to be near Siringo's age, and he seemed to be angry. He wore an eastern business suit of deep blue linen, a white cotton shirt with a starched upright collar, a navy-blue silk tie with a pearl stickpin, and a navy-blue bowler. Silvery-white muttonchops disguised heavy jowls that went along with a robust girth. A bulbous nose latticed with broken capillaries was flanked by coal-black shark's eyes.

The second man gave the appearance of being cool and determined. Younger than his companion by at least a decade, he moved with grace and agility, giving Siringo the impression he knew his way around death, an impression enhanced by the man's attire: black coat, charcoal-gray trousers, spit-shined black boots, white linen shirt with a celluloid collar, black tie tucked inside a gray vest. Only two items—a black bowler cocked to one side of his head, giving him a rakish look, and a Colt .44 with an ivory grip, slung low on his hip and the holster tied to his thigh—kept Siringo from mistaking this man for an undertaker.

As he noted out of the corner of his eye how Beal stiffened at the presence of the new arrivals, the intuition of the detective suggested to Siringo that he linger at the plat map and observe these newcomers interact with the newspaper publisher.

"Beal, I want a word with you," said the older man loudly, his voice demanding as well as commanding attention.

"Good afternoon, Mr. Simpson," said Beal. He glanced in the younger man's direction and added, "Mr. Benteen."

"Never mind the amenities, Beal," growled Simpson. "I haven't the time nor the inclination."

"What can I do for you, Mr. Simpson?" asked Beal, trying to retain a semblance of cordiality.

"You can print a retraction in this rag you have the nerve to call a newspaper." Almost as if by magic, Simpson produced an issue of the *Miner* and began waving it wildly in front of him, somewhat threatening Beal with it.

"A retraction of what, sir?" asked Beal ever so innocently.

"You know perfectly well what, Beal. This damning editorial of yours. This pack of half-truths and exaggerated innuendos. I want you to print the truth."

"You hold the truth in your hand, Mr. Simpson," said Beal.

"You call this truth?" Simpson snapped the paper open and read from it. " 'Shaft No. 8 is a devil's hole, a tunnel straight to Hell for the lowly miner who has the misfortune of being forced to toil in its depths.' " He slapped the tabloid pages together and stuffed them under his left arm. "You call that truth? That, Mr. Beal, is an outright lie!"

"Not according to Hans Friedkin," Beal retaliated.

"Friedkin again!" grumbled Simpson. "That rabble-rouser! Damn that Bolshevik!"

Beal offered a wry smile and said, "Why don't you discharge him if he's so much trouble to you, Mr. Simpson?"

"You know perfectly well why I can't do that, Beal."

"Yes, I do, don't I?"

"Damn you, too, Beal! And damn this newspaper! I'll see you both in ruin before I'm through."

"You're already through, Simpson," said Beal, his demeanor changing as he released some pent-up ire himself. "Only you fail to realize that fact."

"Says you, Beal."

"No, not I, Simpson, but Hans Friedkin and his fellow miners. You exploiters of the working classes have all outlived your day. This is the era of the worker, Simpson, not the slave-driving capitalist. No, sir. I am not the one facing destruction. It is you, Simpson. You and all the bosses who misuse your fellow man. Like the patricians of ancient Rome, you and all the bosses are doomed, are marked for destruction. The workers of the world will grind you to a fine dust, then watch your pitiful remains vanish in the winds of progressive change."

"Progressive change? You sound like that damn reformer Roosevelt. A traitor to his own class. That damn cowboy is nothing more than another Bolshevik!"

"A champion, sir! A hero to the American worker! An inspiration to decent men everywhere! A reformer, yes! A progressive, yes! A Bolshevik? Hardly! A great humani—"

"Never mind any more of your epithets, Beal," interrupted Simpson. "The man is a traitor to his own class. Thank God he's no longer in the White House."

"A void that will be filled at the polls come the November election, I assure you."

"Not if I have anything to do with it!"

"And what can you do, Simpson?" Beal demanded.

Simpson gave the appearance of wanting to answer but didn't. Instead, he smiled briefly, much to Beal's surprise, then frowned and said, "Never you mind, Beal. That is a matter for the future. For the present, I want that retraction or else."

"Are you threatening me, Simpson?" hissed Beal like a cornered cat.

"I have no need to make threats, Beal. In the gambler's terminology, that is called tipping one's hand, and I never tip my hand, Beal. Now print that retraction."

"Never!"

"Is that your final word on the matter, Beal?"

"No, it is not," said Beal, now calmer. "You can read my final word in the next edition of the *Miner.*"

"If there is a next edition," countered Simpson. And with that, he turned and stormed for the door.

Benteen had remained in the background all this time, making absolutely no sounds or movements, not even a shift of his onyx eyes. But as soon as Simpson struck for the exit, he stepped forward and faced Beal directly. Silence resounded between the two men as they stared at each other for the longest moment. Then a smile spread Benteen's thin lips, wrinkling his clean-shaven, pock-marked cheeks. Deliberately, he brushed the butt of his six-gun as he reached up to tip his hat to the publisher.

"It was nice to see you looking so healthy, Mr. Beal," said Benteen. "Until we meet again?"

Beal made no reply, as fear had paralyzed his vocal cords.

Benteen turned and lithely followed Simpson outside.

Siringo thought he recognized something familiar in the final exchange; something younger, out of the past. But where? When? What was there about this man Benteen that suddenly stirred the recesses of his memory?

Whatever it was, it would come to him. In due time.

SIX

Earp's hole card was an ace of hearts. Facing the two players was a spade deuce. Both of them stood pat with two cards each. Earp turned up the sharp-top, then drew an eight of diamonds. Twenty-one. The name of the game.

"That does me in," said the miner who had been betting dimes and quarters. He tossed in his hand and slid his chair away from the table. Rising, he strolled over to the bar and joined a few friends for a glass of beer.

"You're on a streak, Eagan," said the other gambler. He was a bespectacled gent who had an air of refinement and education in everything about him, from his maroon and navy-blue pinstripe suit to his closely cropped graying, thinning hair and clean-shaven face that bore the pallor of a man who worked indoors all the time and worried a lot. His name was Malcolm Caswell and he was the sole proprietor of the Harqua Hala Bank.

"Luck of the draw, Mr. Caswell," said Earp as he swept up the cards and began shuffling the deck.

"And it seems to me that it's all on your side of the table this evening. Well, I've had worse runs of luck, and learning from those experiences, I'm now wise enough to know when to quit. You can cash me in, Eagan."

Caswell pushed a short stack of chips over to Earp, who gave them a quick count before passing back their equivalent in hard cash. The banker then stood and left Earp alone.

The solitude Earp enjoyed only lasted for a few moments. He was soon joined by a new player: a middle-aged, heavily rouged and powdered, overweight lady in a blond wig that failed to take off as many years as she wished. She moved with grace and style in a low-cut dance-hall dress of lavender-and-black satin, the material being her trademark.

"Is this game closed to women?" she asked, her voice a pitch above husky.

Earp merely glanced up at her at first. Then suddenly he realized he was being confronted by a face from his past. An instant, piercing fear of being exposed hackled the hairs on his neck. He tried to disguise the emotion with cool nonchalance.

"If you've got the money," said Earp coldly, "I'll deal the cards."

She sat down and placed a silver dollar in the betting circle painted on the table in front of her. A smile curled her painted lips, and her violet eyes sparkled in Earp's direction, making it impossible for him to ignore her. Most of the youthful loveliness she had possessed in radiant abundance when he knew her in Telluride had been replaced by rounder, fuller features, from her cheeks and chin to her hips and thighs.

"Big George tells me your name is Eagan," she said.

Earp continued to be icy, saying, "That's right. Wade Eagan. Late of Vidal, California."

"Never heard of it," she said, "but I'm still glad to make your acquaintance, Mr. Eagan. I'm Mamie Sattin. My girls and I rent the rooms upstairs."

"How do you do, Mamie? It's always good to know the other working people in an establishment. Would you permit me to buy you a drink?"

"Only if you'll let me return the favor. Later. In my room. Where we can get better acquainted."

"Well, thank you, Mamie, for the invite," said Earp, forcing a smile for the first time. "But it's always been a practice of mine not to . . . fraternize with the other workers. That way they don't get to expecting me to deal them winners every time they sit down at my table."

"I hadn't planned to fraternize, Wade," said Mamie almost testily. "Just a little social meeting is all I had in mind. A drink and a little conversation. Polite conversation. Kind of get to know each other. After all, since we're working under the same roof, we should get better acquainted, don't you think? And I've got a feeling we just might have a lot in common . . . if you know what I mean."

"I think I do, Mamie. You could be right about that. Maybe we should get better acquainted. Should I come up as soon as I close down for the night?"

"Sure, you do that. I'll be waiting." She stood, picking up the silver cartwheel she had put down for a bet. "Now don't forget, Wade. I'm sure we'll have lots to talk about."

SEVEN

Instead of going up to see Mamie Sattin straightaway after closing down his game for the night, Earp returned to the Gold House for a meeting with Siringo. The former Pinkerton detective was waiting patiently in his own room when Earp tapped out their previously arranged signal on the wall that separated their lodgings. Siringo knuckled an answering code, then joined Earp in his room.

"How was your game?" Siringo asked at the top of the conversation. He straddled the lone wooden straight-back chair.

Earp used his left hand to neatly fold two short stacks of silver dollars into one large column next to him on the bed; this was a nervous habit of professional gamblers and dealers. He repeated the action as he said, "Lot of nickel-and-dimers around here. Only thing close to a high-roller was the banker. One Malcolm Caswell. Dropped about fifteen bucks, then pulled out. Rest were miners and one a teamster. I guess I cleared twenty-five or so." He chuckled and added, "I got an oil well over on the Coast that makes me more than that in an hour."

"Is that so? Oil well, you say? Wish I had a couple. Writing books about the old days keeps the bills paid but not much else. What with automobiles and now aeroplanes, oil is the coming thing. Fortunes are already being made. And you say you got one?"

"Sally and me own part of a whole field of oil wells," said Earp casually.

"A whole field? Then why on earth do you two run around the desert looking for gold and silver all the time? Especially when you've got that kind of money."

Earp shrugged and said, "Sometimes I wonder that myself, Charlie. Best answer I've got is we like the peace and privacy. When we're in the city—Los Angeles or San Francisco—we're never left alone. Someone is always inviting us to something or another. Everyone wants to have the famous gunfighter over for dinner or to a ball or something. Damn that Ned Buntline!"

"Now there's a name I haven't heard in years. Ned Buntline. He sure did a lot for Bill Cody, didn't he?"

"That only shows you what a liar Buntline was. Buffalo Bill!" Earp practically spat the name. "The great Indian fighter! Custer's avenger! Pure bunkum, Charlie, and all trumped up by Buntline and those other eastern writers who never set a foot west of Chicago."

"And now the moving pictures are doing the same thing," said Siringo. "I saw a moving-picture show in Dallas called *The Great Train Robbery*. I got to admit it was exciting. Not a whole lot like the real thing, but when you don't know any better, it was downright thrilling."

"Sure, I heard about that," said Earp. "Some newspaper writer stopped me on a street in Los Angeles last spring and asked me what I thought about that moving picture. I told him I hadn't seen it and that I had no intentions of ever seeing it. I told him I'd had my fill of the lawless West."

"So that's why you're here in Harqua Hala?"

Earp permitted a grudging smile. "Well, maybe I haven't quite had my fill yet." He chuckled again and said, "I got a little reminder of what the old days were like this afternoon. I had a little run-in with the new deputy. I wonder if Farnsworth knows that his man is a young hothead with a chip on his shoulder and just daring some other young hothead to come knock it off. His name is Jake Poole. Thought he could push an old goat like me around in public. But we got to talking more peaceably after we came to an understanding about manners and respect for one's elders and betters, I might add."

"Did he say anything about Walt?"

"Only that Phillips was shot while making his rounds one night in June. I asked him if he had any leads on who did it, and just like Farnsworth, he didn't have a clue. From the looks of him, I don't think he would know a clue even if it bit him in his hinder parts."

"A bit slow on the draw, eh?" said Siringo with a slight snicker.

"You might say that," said Earp. "He almost got a real fight going. This young tinhorn almost stuck his nose in it while I was teaching Poole some courtesy. Speaking of him, his name is Patton —George Patton. He's a civil engineer . . . or so he says. He told me he's here to see about laying out some more roads and building a few bridges around these parts. If you ask me, I can't see that any more roads and bridges are needed around here. What's more, he carries a piece in a shoulder holster. I felt it when I bumped into him in the lobby this morning. Then I thought I saw him start to go for it when Poole and me were having our little lesson. He's got the room on the other side of you, Charlie. I think we might be wise to keep an eye on him."

"You don't suppose Farnsworth called in the Pinkertons, do you, Wyatt?"

"No, I don't think Farnsworth would do that without telling us. Besides, we just got started. He wouldn't bring in an outsider just yet. Especially an Easterner. No, I don't think Patton is a Pinkerton. He's too green to be a Pinkerton man."

"I'll take a look at him tomorrow," said Siringo.

"Do that, and maybe you can figure out why he's hiding who he really is or what he really is. Now what about you? How did your day go? Buy any ranches today?"

"No, but I did meet a couple of interesting types this afternoon. The newspaper is run by a skinny little needle-nosed runt named Horace Beal. Seems like every Horace I've ever met was a runt. Anyway, I got the feeling that he knows more than he lets on. All he could tell me about the killing was what we already know. Then there was this other fellow. A businessman named Simpson. I gathered he's a bigwig with the mining company, the way he carried on. He came into the newspaper all abluster and had an argument with Beal over some editorial.

"But it wasn't Simpson who interested me so much as it was the fellow with him. I think Beal called him Benteen. I can't put my finger on it yet, but there was something familiar about him. I know him from somewhere, but I can't rightly recollect where. There was this glint in his eye that reminded me of someone, but I can't remember who it is."

"You ran too many men to ground, Charlie," said Earp with a wry smile.

Siringo grinned and said, "Well, I didn't catch them all, Wyatt. Most. But not all."

"Well, you'll remember who this Benteen reminds you of, sooner or later."

"You're probably right, Wyatt. Still it's bothering me. Something else is bothering me, too. Did Farnsworth say anything to you about Walt owning a mining claim?"

"Mining claim? No, can't say that he did. Where'd you find that out?"

"At the newspaper office. Beal provided me with a plat map that had all the landowners' names on them. And while I was listening to him have a row with Simpson, I came across Walt's name on the map. Not just once, but in eight places. It seems he staked out a few claims in the area when he wasn't upholding the law."

"And maybe he was working those claims on his days off," said Earp suddenly. "And maybe that explains something Farnsworth couldn't explain—why Phillips had so much money in the bank when he died."

"You didn't say anything about that before."

"I didn't think it was important. Farnsworth was puzzled by it, but he didn't make any fuss over it either."

"How much did he have in the bank?"

"Close to five thousand, said Farnsworth."

"Five thousand? And you don't find that kind of peculiar? Good Lord, man! Five thousand dollars is a lot of money . . . especially for a sheriff's deputy. Where would a deputy sheriff get that kind of money?"

"Maybe he was gambling and winning a lot. Or maybe he was working his claims. How would I know?" Earp was a bit testy.

"Well, maybe we better just find out where he got the money," Siringo suggested.

"And how do we go about that? Neither you nor me can go in to banker Caswell and ask him about Walt's account at the bank. Not without giving ourselves away."

"We send a letter to Farnsworth and have him do it. And when he finds out, maybe we'll have a lead on why someone killed Walt in the middle of the night."

"You could be right, Charlie. Maybe the money is the place to start looking for Walt's killer."

"Okay, first thing tomorrow I'll send off a telegram to Farnsworth. But maybe I'd better go back to Salome to do it. No telling who we can trust around here."

"Speaking of trust, Charlie," said Earp with a bit of worry showing on his tired features, "we got us a problem."

"A problem?"

"Mamie Sattin."

Siringo's eyes squinted involuntarily as he tried to place a face with the name. "Mamie Sattin?" he said softly.

"Telluride," said Earp, helping to jog Siringo's memory. "About twenty years back."

"A real looker? With a beauty mark shaped like a heart on the right side of her chin?" He pointed to his own jaw to indicate where he meant.

"That's the one," said Earp. "Only now she doesn't have that beauty mark. She's a lot plumper than back then, too."

"Did she recognize you?" asked Siringo.

"I think so," said Earp, frowning, "but she didn't call me by my right name."

"She played along?"

"She did. For the moment."

"For the moment? What does that mean?"

Earp looked a little embarrassed and said, "She invited me up to her room for a drink and a little social chat."

"Did you go?"

"Not yet. I told her I'd come up after I closed down for the night."

"Well, what are you doing here? There's a lady waiting!"

"I thought I'd better check in with you first, Charlie. Besides, I'm not sure what I should tell her when she asks me why I'm here under an assumed name."

"Why don't you tell her the truth?" Siringo offered.

"The truth?"

"That's right. Tell her the truth. There's no sense lying to her. Sooner or later, she's going to see me, and although she might not recognize me, we can't afford to take that chance. Tell her everything, and she just might help us. After all, she didn't give you away in the saloon, did she?"

"I suppose you're right, Charlie. Who knows? Mamie just might put us onto something. Okay, I'll give her a go."

EIGHT

Mamie's room had the look of a woman who had graduated from working in the business to running it. Satin and lace seemed to be everywhere. Purple pillows with pink trim were strewn on a canopied bed that was covered by a white spread imprinted with blue and violet flowers and enhanced with matching curtains. A lavender dresser scarf adorned the dressing table, and mirrors and glass-framed pictures were hung on the papered walls, whose design reminded the viewer of irises in full bloom. Crocheted doilies—creamy-white snowflake patterns inset with lilacs—daintily caressed the arms of two sitting-room chairs that were upholstered with maroon damask. Only an array of liquor bottles and crystal drinking glasses atop the chiffonier betrayed the chamber's class, stating quite frankly that it was not the boudoir of an elegant lady.

When Mamie answered his knock at the door, Earp was pleased to find her still entirely clothed, a statement that their meeting promised to be exactly what she said it would be. Upon seeing the decor, he removed his hat and waited for Mamie to offer him a chair and seat herself before he would sit down.

"Well, Mr. Wade Eagan," said Mamie with her hands folded primly in her lap, "I was beginning to think you weren't coming. After all, you closed down your game almost an hour ago."

"I returned to my hotel room for a moment," stammered Earp. Then hastily, he added, "To refresh myself before calling on a lady."

"But, of course. Now about that drink." She stood and glided over to the dresser. "Bourbon?"

Mamie poured the whiskey, two fingers worth, into a tumbler, then did the same with a bottle of gin in another glass. She handed Earp his drink and took hers back to her seat.

"To days gone by," said Mamie, raising her glass in Earp's direction.

Earp returned the toast and said, "To the days ahead." They

drank, then merely sat for a moment, staring at each other, wondering what to say. Finally, Earp shifted his gaze to a picture of Mamie when she was twenty years younger.

"I once knew a girl who looked like that," said Earp. "A working girl. It was said you could trust her to keep your business so secret that she wouldn't even tell you what you were doing."

"That's still true," said Mamie. "That's why we're playing this charade, isn't it?"

"Then you know?" Earp was not astounded, only mildly surprised, more by the fact that he had guessed right than that she had recognized him.

"From the first moment I saw you at your table. Big George pointed you out to me, but before I could say anything, he told me your name was Eagan. So I thought I'd keep quiet until we had a chance to talk."

"That was mighty nice obliging of you, Mamie," said Earp, relieved. "I suppose you'll be wanting an explanation."

"Only if you wish to give me one, Wyatt. I'm sure you have your reasons for being here under an assumed name. It's my guess it has something to do with that Tombstone business way back when."

"No, Mamie, it's not that. Most of those involved in that affair are long since dead and more than likely forgotten. No, it's not that, Mamie. I'm not hiding from the law."

Mamie smiled and leaned forward. "Now you have roused my curiosity. If you're not running from the law, then there must be a woman involved. Is that it?"

Earp couldn't stop a grin from lighting up his face. "No, Mamie, it's not that either. I'm flattered that you would think so, but that isn't it. It's Walt Phillips."

A sou'wester blew up in Mamie's eyes for an instant, only to be replaced just as quickly by placid control. In the double blink of Earp's eyelids, she had changed from honest curiosity to troubled concern to feigned disinterest.

"Walt . . . Phillips? He's dead."

"I know," said Earp. "That's why I'm here. To find out who killed him. Me and . . . Charlie Siringo."

"The Pinkerton?"

"He thought you'd remember him."

"Is he using a different name, too? He must be. Someone like him would hardly go unnoticed around here for very long."

"Yes, he is. Clayton Stewart, that's him. He's posing as a cattle rancher from Texas."

"But why not use your real names?" asked Mamie.

"Clyde Farnsworth tried that, didn't he? And where did it get him? He told me he knew less when he left here than when he came. So Charlie and I figured folks hereabouts wouldn't be any more willing to talk to Wyatt Earp and Charlie Siringo than they were to Farnsworth. But they might be willing to talk to Wade Eagan and Clayton Stewart, a couple of old-timers appearing to be perfectly harmless. Only thing is, we didn't figure on running into anyone from the old days."

"Meaning me?"

"Meaning you. Farnsworth didn't mention you, so you were quite a surprise to me this evening. Anyone else around here from the old days?"

"No one I know about," said Mamie. "But you can never tell. All sorts of drifters come through here looking to make a fast buck or two. Not many do, though. This is not a fast town, Wyatt. Now with statehood and those do-gooders putting an end to all the fun in life, it's worse. Did you know they made this a dry state?" She laughed and added, "As if Arizona isn't dry enough already."

Earp couldn't suppress a grin, saying, "So true, so true." Then turning serious again, he asked, "What do you know about it, Mamie? The shooting, I mean. It's apparent Farnsworth didn't question you or he would have mentioned it to me."

"No, he never asked me a thing about it, and I didn't volunteer nothing. No one would have believed anything I had to say anyway."

"Well, I'll believe you, Mamie," said Earp sincerely. "You can tell me what you know about the killing."

Mamie stood up and walked slowly to the window. She peered through the black glass, looking down at the dark streets and alleys of the town, her expression sad and lonely.

"It happened right down there," she said. "Down there, around the corner of the jail. That's where old Walt was found." The tone of her voice matched the look on her face. "It was late. Around one in the morning or so. I was just starting to undress when I heard the first shot."

"The first shot?" queried Earp. "I was told there was only one shot. Are you saying there were two?"

"That's right. Two. I heard the first one and ran to the window just in time to see the blast of the second one. Whoever it was that killed Walt was standing in the alley between the newspaper building and Mrs. Gianelli's boardinghouse. Here. Take a look."

Earp joined her by the window.

"See?" Mamie pointed below. "That's the rear of the newspaper building, and over there is Mrs. Gianelli's. The jail is right next door."

Earp peeked out and said, "Then what happened?"

"Then someone down in the saloon yelled something about hearing gunfire, and pretty soon there were men all over down there. I kept watching from up here. A couple of boys brought out some lanterns to look around, and in a minute or so, they found Walt. My window was open just like it is now, and I heard someone shout, 'Somebody's shot Walt Phillips!' I put on a robe and ran downstairs. They were just bringing his body through the back door. Somebody yelled to get a doctor, and they put him on a couple of tables pushed together by two of my girls. He was already dead. There was so much blood it was hard to tell where he'd been shot. It wasn't till after the undertaker got him all cleaned up for the funeral that we learned he'd been shot in the chest."

"You say you saw the second shot," said Earp. "Did you see who it was doing the shooting?"

"It was too dark to make out anything. There was no moon that night. Whoever it was could have run off in any of six different directions and no one would have seen him."

"But it seems to me," said Earp, "that someone would have noticed a man carrying a shotgun running away from a shooting."

"It was pitch black, Wyatt. I couldn't see a thing till they brought out the lanterns."

Mamie returned to the chiffonier and poured herself another drink. She held up the bottle of bourbon toward Earp as if to ask him if he wanted a refill, but he shook his head negatively, his thoughts on what to ask her next. Mamie replaced the bottle, then sat down again.

Still standing by the window, Earp asked, "What happened then?"

"Not much. Jake Poole, Walt's deputy, or he was then. That no-account was always trying to get Walt to quit so he could take his place, and that's just what happened when Walt got killed. Now he's got the job he's wanted for so long. Walt's job."

"Do you think Poole could have killed Walt for his job?"

"You don't know Jake Poole, do you, Wyatt?"

"We had the occasion to meet earlier today."

"Do you think he's got enough backbone to kill anyone? Even in cold blood in the dark?"

Earp studied on the question for a moment, then said, "I see what you mean. No, Poole seems to lack the killer instinct. Even so, I'll keep him in mind. But you started to say something about Poole on the night Walt was killed."

"Oh, yeah, I did. Right after someone figured out Walt was dead, Poole came busting through the front door, sweating like he'd just run a long race and lost. He started organizing a posse to search the town, but before he could, Big George came in and talked some sense into everyone. He said it was too dark to search, and besides, the killer was long gone by now. Better to wait till morning and have a good look at the place where Walt was shot. Poole saw the sense in that and told everyone to stay out of the alley until he had a chance to take a look around in the morning. So they took Walt's body over to the undertaker's, then Big George closed up the place."

"Back up there a piece, Mamie," said Earp. "You said Big George came in and talked some sense into everyone. Wasn't Big George there in the bar in the beginning?"

Mamie looked perplexed for moment, then shaking her head, she said, "Come to think of it, I didn't see him when I came downstairs, and I don't remember seeing him out back when they brought the lanterns out. And another thing. I don't recall him wearing his apron when he came into the bar from the back room. That's funny. Big George always wears his apron in the bar. The only time he takes it off is when he goes out somewhere or when he goes to bed."

"That makes two men who can't be accounted for at the time Walt was shot down," said Earp. "Now I'm wondering who else wasn't where they should have been at that time. Was there anyone else around that night who shouldn't have been? Or anyone who should have been and wasn't?"

"Nobody I can think of right off. Just Poole and Big George. And as far as who was in the saloon that night, I don't recall anyone who wouldn't have been there normally at that time of night."

"What about earlier in the evening? Was there anyone around who didn't normally come into the Dutchman's? Or did anything unusual happen that evening?"

"Yeah, there was. Two or three hours before the shooting, Walt and Jake came upstairs to break up a ruckus between Ardmore Simpson and Hans Friedkin."

"Simpson? Charlie mentioned him just before I came up here to see you. Simpson is some kind of bit shot with the mining company, isn't he?"

"Ardmore Simpson owns the Harqua Hala Mining Company. He was visiting one of my girls that night when Friedkin came upstairs as drunk as a Texas cowboy on a two-week binge after a four-month cattle drive."

"Who is this Friedkin?" asked Earp.

"Friedkin is Simpson's blaster, not to mention Number One Troublemaker. He's been trying to organize a union of the miners, and Simpson has been doing everything he can to stop him. He came here about six months ago, some say straight off the boat from Germany, but I don't think so. His lingo is too good. Speaks American so good you'd hardly know he was a foreigner. He calls himself a labor organizer, but Simpson calls him a Bolshevik, whatever that is. Horace Beal—he's the newspaper publisher—he calls him a champion of the working class, whatever *that* means. It's all politics and malarkey to me."

"So Friedkin came up here and broke in on Simpson and one of your girls and Walt and Jake Poole came up to break it up. Then what happened?"

"I tried to get Friedkin to leave first, but he wouldn't listen to me. Big George came up before Walt and Poole, but Friedkin was too drunk to be scared by him. George was about to throw him out when Walt and Poole finally showed. George let Friedkin go, and that hothead gave him a cheap shot on the chin and knocked Big George on his can. Big George was fighting mad then. But Walt— Did you know Walt very well?"

"No, I didn't," said Earp.

"Then why—"

"Because Clyde Farnsworth asked me to," said Earp, anticipating her question.

"I see. Well, Walt stepped between Big George and Friedkin, but Big George wasn't going to be stopped from getting a piece of Friedkin. At least he wasn't till Walt pulled his gun and shoved it in his face. Big George told Walt to stay out of it and started to take one more step, but Walt told him if he made another move he'd blow his head off. He meant it, too. And Big George knew it. He was still mad when Walt took Friedkin away in handcuffs."

"And what about Simpson all this time?" asked Earp.

"Poole saw to it that Simpson got out the back way without anyone seeing him. Poole's a bootlicker, and he's been making up to Simpson ever since Simpson's daughter came to town. So he got Simpson out of sight real quick. Can't have one of the pillars of the community seen in a place like this, if you know what I mean. Simpson's a churchgoer and all that do-gooder malarkey. But I know better, and so do a lot of others. He sneaks up here once or twice a month or so. Pays the girls right good to keep their mouths shut about it."

"Is he married?"

"No, a widower. Had his daughter off at some eastern ladies' school up to about six months ago. New York, I think. Simpson told one of my girls about it. Said his daughter got herself mixed up with some man and got herself thrown out of school. That's about all I know about it."

"You seem to know quite a lot about everything, Mamie," said Earp. "I know a lot more now about Walt's murder than I did this morning. But I'm still pretty green at this detective business, and I don't know what all I should be asking you. So I think it would be better if you talked to Charlie."

"Sure, Wyatt. When?"

"Tomorrow night maybe. I'll have him come in and play a few hands at my table. You come around and—"

"I know just what to do from there, Wyatt."

"One last question, Mamie. Got any ideas about who else besides Jake Poole and Big George might have wanted Walt Phillips dead?"

"Sure," she said with a huff. Then she looked away from Earp toward the window again, her face limp and lost.

"Who?"

"Me."

NINE

The sun was already at its zenith when Earp awakened to face the day, but by that time Siringo had ridden to Salome and back and was sitting in the office of Malcolm Caswell at the Harqua Hala Bank.

"I have considerable funds," Siringo was saying, "back in Dallas, Mr. Caswell. Enough to finance all my proposed acquisitions and operations here in Arizona. What I am looking for is a secure bank —a bank secure enough to protect my money until such time that I need it."

"Rest assured, Mr. Stewart," said Caswell eagerly and with all the creamy tones he could muster, "this institution is as safe as any in the state."

"That is what worries me, sir. I've seen several banks in this state, and none of them have satisfied my rather stringent requirements for safety."

"I assure you, Mr. Stewart—"

"Never mind your assurances, Mr. Caswell. Words, that's all your assurances are. Cheap talk. You, sir, are a stranger to me, as I am to you, and that makes your word, as well as my own, totally worthless. That may be blunt, sir, but it's honest. I want none of your verbal assurances. I wish to see the security of this bank with my own eyes."

Caswell was unaccustomed to having anyone speak rudely to him, and it showed in his color: ashen gray. But he recovered quickly.

"Certainly, Mr. Stewart," he said obediently. "A tour of the premises. Is that your pleasure, sir?"

"That will do for starters." Siringo stood, dwarfing Caswell. He looked around the room. "Tell me, sir. What protection do you have in here should there be a robbery in the area of the teller's cage?"

Caswell was mentally unhorsed by the question, and his expression betrayed his lack of an appropriate answer.

"But . . . but," Caswell stammered, breaking out in a cold, cowardly sweat, "if the robbery is in the outer office, why would I need protection in here?"

"Who has the combination to your safe, Mr. Caswell?"

"Combi . . . safe?"

"Come, come, man! Who has the combination to your safe?"

"Why, I do, of course."

"And who else?"

Caswell was absolutely dumbfounded and totally perplexed by this string of questions. But still, he said, "No one else. Just I have it."

"Precisely my point," said Siringo.

"Precisely, Mr. Stewart?"

"Precisely, Mr. Caswell. Don't you see it? If you are in here and a robbery is taking place outside and the safe is locked, the robbers would have to come in here to get you to open the safe. Isn't that so?"

The dawn of understanding shone on Caswell's face. "Yes, yes! Now I see your point. If the robbers can't get to me, they can't get to the money. That's it, isn't it?"

"Precisely, sir."

Caswell suddenly appeared confused again. "But what can be done to ensure my safety within these walls?"

"First," said Siringo, wagging a finger at the surrounding area, then at Caswell, "you replace all that frosted glass with wood and steel. Steel for practicality, and wood for show. The same for the door. And the door—that is the key to your safety. It should have double bolts on the inside and should be locked whenever you are in here during business hours."

Caswell was astounded. Thoughts such as these had never crossed his mind before, and now a total stranger was telling him how to protect himself and the funds of his depositors. He was aghast. So much so that he sat rigid and disbelieving.

"Don't just sit there, man!" snapped Siringo. "Write this down and see that it gets done or my money will never reside in this place."

"Yes . . . yes, of course." Caswell fumbled for a pen and paper, found both, then began writing furiously. As soon as he had finished, he looked up at Siringo and asked, "What other suggestions do you have, Mr. Stewart?"

Siringo pointed and said, "Replace that window with a door just like the one I've already described. That way, you could escape to inform the authorities immediately of the robbery as it is happening."

"Very clever, sir." He began to write down the suggestion but stopped in midsentence. "But if I am locked in here, how will I know a robbery is taking place in the outer office?"

"Some sort of signal system will have to be installed. A simple battery-powered bell would suffice."

Caswell resumed writing. "Yes, of course. A bell."

"And now, the safe," said Siringo, making it sound like a command.

"The safe?" asked Caswell, looking up from the paper.

"The safe. Where is it?"

"Why, it's in the back."

"Well?"

Caswell was on his feet in an instant and on his way to the door, opening it, then standing aside to permit Siringo to pass through the portal first. "Right this way, Mr. Stewart."

Siringo stood with all the stateliness of an English lord, paused to straighten his suit, then proceeded to exit the office. He turned toward the rear of the building and walked in the direction of the safe. Caswell closed the door behind them, then scurried past Siringo to lead the way. They came to another door, and Caswell opened it for his guest. Siringo stepped inside the room, which was furnished with a plain wooden table and two matching chairs. A kerosene lamp, providing tolerable illumination, enough so to create gray shadows instead of black, sat mournfully alone in the middle of the table. The walk-in safe occupied the wall opposite the door, and the other walls were bare. Looking up, Siringo noted a four-foot crawl space between the safe and the slat ceiling. Caswell remained at the doorway.

"As you can see, Mr. Stewart," said Caswell, "we have one of the latest models. I had it shipped all the—"

"Open it," said Siringo.

"Open it? But why? I assure you—"

Siringo turned slowly and glared at Caswell, causing the banker to break off in midsentence. It was the command Caswell needed. He opened the safe.

"Bring the lamp," said Siringo. "I want to look inside."

Caswell didn't hesitate, carrying out the order with expedience and efficiency.

Siringo had to stoop to get into and look around the vault. One side of it was occupied by safe-deposit boxes. The opposite side and back wall had shelves, and on these were stacks of banded greenbacks and several bulging coin bags.

"How much do you have here?" asked Siringo.

"Roughly seventeen thousand in cash," said Caswell.

"Your total assets?"

"Heavens, no! We have much more than that sum in stocks and bonds and collateral. Our assets total almost one hundred thousand dollars."

"Almost?" queried Siringo. "You mean you don't know exactly?"

"Well . . . no." Before Siringo could ask, Caswell anticipated the next question and said, "But I can find out in just one minute." And with that, he rushed out of the safe.

Suddenly being left alone, Siringo felt a slight embarrassment and nervously thumbed a packet of bills. He noted the top one was a twenty, but those beneath it were lacking printing and government green. Curious now, he ruffled another and discovered it to be the same: a twenty on top and plain paper cut to the dimensions of currency under it. He checked a third with the same result. Then a fourth and fifth. All alike. His eye set on the coin bags. He hefted one. It was heavy enough, but when he replaced it, the sound wasn't right. He felt it. The contents weren't coin of the realm. Gold nuggets? He opened the sack and peered inside. Rocks!

The tattoo of Caswell's boots on the wooden floor outside the safe prevented Siringo from giving any further thought to the bogus money. He quickly retied the string, then backed away from the shelf.

Caswell stepped into the repository and said, "The bank's assets total—"

Siringo waved him off. "Getting me an exact figure was quite unnecessary, Mr. Caswell."

"Well, I . . ." The banker broke off when he saw Siringo reach for his pocket watch.

Siringo checked the hour, then said, "Mr. Caswell, I have taken up too much of your time and mine. As soon as you have made the alterations to this establishment, I will have my bank in Dallas transfer my funds here. Good day, sir."

TEN

Patton stopped his Hupmobile in front of the Gold House and switched off the magneto. After lifting his driving goggles over the visor of his tan porkpie, he climbed out of the auto, removed his gauntlets, then slapped the road dirt from his linen duster with the gloves. Satisfied that the coat was clean enough, he took it off, turned it inside out, folded it up neatly, and placed it under the driver's seat. He put the hat and eyewear in the same place.

The engineer then went to the rear of the car and opened the trunk. He took out a towel and walked over to a horse trough at the shady side of the building. He dipped one corner of the cloth into the water, then washed half a pound of Arizona real estate from his face and neck. Once the dirt was gone, he moistened the rest of the towel and wiped himself again; the cool wet feeling good, refreshing him from the desert heat. Clean now, Patton washed out the towel, then returned to the Hupmobile's trunk.

As Patton folded and replaced the washcloth, Earp came out of the hotel and approached the younger man. He stopped at the corner of the short boardwalk and leaned against the veranda post.

"I didn't know you had one of these things, George," said Earp. "You don't see too many automobiles out here in the West. Except maybe over in Los Angeles or up in San Francisco. They got quite a few over there."

"You've been in those cities quite recently, I take it," said Patton. Still suspicious that this new acquaintance wasn't exactly what he seemed, the engineer eyed Earp closely, looking for some sign from the older man that might give him away.

Without a blink, Earp replied, "Yes, I was in Los Angeles recently. Before coming here, I went to San Francisco to look up some old friends and found out they had moved to southern California. So I went to Los Angeles, but after looking for them for a month and with my poke running low, I decided it was time to find a place to set up a game. The mining camps here in Arizona seemed best at the time, so here I am. Course, now I ain't so sure it was the right thing."

"What makes you say that?"

"Arizona doesn't appear to be as prosperous these days as it was in the past. Seems to me there are more folks leaving this place than there are moving here."

"Then you've been here before?" asked Patton.

"Not here in Harqua Hala," replied Earp. "But in Arizona, yes. Been a few years, though. I was pretty young back then."

"When was that?"

"Let me see now," said Earp, scratching at his chin as if the action would stir his memory. "Must be thirty, thirty-five years or so. Somewhere around that. Spent a little time in Prescott, then moved on to Tombstone."

"Tombstone?" Patton said the name with honest awe. "You must have known—" Patton stopped short, suddenly realizing that the man he was about to mention had the same initials as the one with whom he was at that very moment conversing. Instead of saying Wyatt Earp, he substituted Earp's late friend. "Uh, Doc Holliday."

Earp was quick to catch Patton's near-gaffe and just as quick to realize that he had better change the subject fast. He ignored Patton's remark and said, "This place is nothing like the old mining towns. Pretty quiet here."

"Yes, Harqua Hala is a dying town," said Patton.

Earp seized upon the opening the younger man had given him by mistake. "Then why are you here, George? If Harqua Hala is dying, why would anyone want to build better roads around here?"

Patton was trapped, and he knew it. He permitted himself an inner snicker at his own expense. The old fox had cornered the hound pup.

"Good question, Wade," said Patton. Then he scanned the immediate vicinity to make certain no one else was within earshot. Although satisfied that they would not be overheard, Patton still took the double precaution of lowering his voice and moving closer to his listener. "Maybe we should talk in private, Wade—if that is your *real* name."

Earp was unshaken. In a level tone, he said, "Yes, maybe we should talk in private, George—if that is *your* real name."

Patton smiled and said, "I'll get my hat, and we can go for a walk."

As Patton returned to the Hupmobile, Earp saw Siringo hurrying up the street toward the hotel. Siringo's gait seemed to Earp to be fueled by urgency.

"George, maybe we should put off that walk for a while," said Earp. "We can talk later."

Patton donned a wide-brimmed peak hat, then glanced up at Earp, noting immediately that the older man's focus was aimed down the street. He shifted his own view accordingly, saw Siringo approaching, and wondered what the connection might be between the older men.

"Maybe your friend might like to join us," said Patton on another fishing trip.

"My friend?" queried Earp.

"He must be your friend. Why else would the two of you be up half the night talking in your room?"

Earp considered Patton's words, then said, "He might at that, but let me have a word with him first."

Earp went to meet Siringo. As they neared each other, Siringo behaved as if he would walk right past Earp, still playing his role as Clayton Stewart the rancher, who ostensibly did not know Wade Eagan the gambler. This would not do for Earp, so he stepped in front of Siringo and halted his friend's progress.

"Hold on, Charlie," he said, forgetting himself.

Surprised by Earp's action and seeing Patton close at hand, Siringo could only react by saying, "Pardon me, sir, is there something I can do for you?"

"I think he's on to us," said Earp a little more conspiratorially. Siringo glanced over Earp's shoulder at Patton. "Who? That young fellow by the automobile?"

"That's him. George Patton. I told you about him. He's playing cat-and-mouse games with his words. I think he knows who I am."

"What if he does?" asked Siringo.

"He could tell someone, and before you know it, the whole town will know. Folks are suspicious enough. If they find out Wyatt Earp is here pretending he's someone else, they'll start wondering why. Then what about you? He knows about our meeting last night."

"Are you saying we should take him into our confidence?"

"I think that will be best. I get the impression he's honest and a straight arrow. We tell him who we are and what we're doing here, and just maybe he'll level with us. I can't see how we have much choice."

"Okay, Wyatt, I'll trust your judgment on this one."

Earp scanned the area, trying to appear as casual as possible, and saw only a few people out in the heat. But he couldn't see into the darkened buildings. There was no telling how many pairs of eyes were watching them.

"Shake hands with me, Charlie," said Earp, offering a friendly grip. "We'd best keep up this charade for the sake of anyone peeping about." They shook. "Come on. I'll introduce you to young Mr. Patton."

The two men sauntered over to Patton, and Earp made the introductions, using Siringo's alias. They chatted briefly about the weather and Patton's vehicle.

"Mechanization, gentlemen," said Patton. "That's the wave of the future. The horse, a beautiful animal that has served man so well since the beginning of recorded history, is soon to become a conveyance of leisure instead of necessity. Even the military will be mechanized before too long. Wars of the future will be fought with machines, not men."

"But men will have to run those machines," said Earp.

"Quite true in the beginning," said Patton, "but the time will come when men will run their machines from a distance. With the advances in science, the wireless telegraph specifically, men will be able to remain in comparable safety and direct their machines to do battle from afar."

Siringo became absorbed in Patton's futuristic discourse and forgot their real purpose for the moment. He laughed and said, "Honestly, Mr. Patton, I believe you've been reading too many Jules Verne novels. Why—"

"Mock me and Mr. Verne if you will, Mr. Stewart, but already Mr. Verne's prediction of undersea travel in iron ships has come about. You are aware of the submarine, aren't you?"

"The submarine?" queried Siringo.

"Yes, the submarine, a ship that travels beneath the waves, unseen by surface ships and capable of delivering a deathblow to even the greatest of the 'Great White Fleet.' A single torpedo launched from a submarine could sink an unsuspecting battleship in a mere matter of minutes."

"You seem to know a great deal about modern warfare," said Earp. "Your occupation, George?"

"Very deductive, uh, Wade," said Patton with a congenial smile. "Well, I suppose it's time we took our little walk and continue the conversation we began earlier."

"Precisely," said Siringo.

They started up Gold Street, three men on a leisurely afternoon stroll.

"I think I've figured out who you are, uh, Wade," said Patton at the top of their resumed dialogue. "Or may I address you as Wyatt?"

"How did you figure out who I am?" asked Earp.

"It didn't come to me at first. Actually, I saw something familiar in your face when we first met. Now I know what it was. I'd seen a printed woodcut of you in an old copy of *Frank Leslie's Illustrated Newspaper.*"

Earp smiled and said, "Yes, I recall that now. Becker, Joseph Becker was the artist. He sketched my brothers and me at the Tombstone trial. I didn't know about it until a year later up in Telluride when some dude walked in and showed me the paper. I didn't think so at the time, but the dude said Becker had done me justice and caught my likeness almost perfectly. Now with you recalling the same picture, I suppose he was right."

"Well, it wasn't until a few minutes ago when you mentioned Tombstone," said Patton, "that I caught on to the name. The initials being the same was the tip-off."

"Then you should be able to figure quite easily who I am," said Siringo.

Patton studied Siringo's face and considered the initials of his alias. "C.S.," said Patton. "I'm sorry—"

"If I said Pinkerton's Detective Agency," said Siringo, "would that help?"

"Pinkerton? You? C.S.?" Then somewhat unsure, he queried, "Siringo? Charles Siringo? The man who ran Butch Cassidy and the Sundance Kid out of the country?"

"I wasn't the only one chasing them," said Siringo.

Suddenly, there was a transformation in Patton. He was no longer the confident, educated engineer but had become an idolizing youth, awed by the company in which it was his distinct pleasure to be walking.

"I'm finding this hard to believe," said Patton. "I've read so much about both of you—"

"Don't believe all you read," said Earp. "I've seen some of those fanciful accounts of my younger days. Mostly tripe, especially that one about how I never drew down on a man with the intent to kill him but did so out of self-defense. I'll tell you this, George . . . By the way, is that your real name?"

"Yes, it is. Lieutenant George Patton, United States Army, Eighth Cavalry, stationed at Fort Huachuca."

"An Army officer?" queried Siringo. "What are you doing here impersonating a civil engineer?"

"I was wondering the same of you two," said Patton. "Why are you using names other than your own?"

"We're here to find out who murdered Deputy Sheriff Walt Phillips," said Earp. "Sheriff Farnsworth from Yuma brought us into this action, and we thought it best to have secret identities when we started asking questions."

"I see," said Patton. "Folks might be a little more willing to talk to two casual strangers than they would to two famous men such as Wyatt Earp and Charles Siringo."

"That's the ticket," said Earp.

"But you haven't answered my question, Lieutenant," said Siringo. "Why are you impersonating a civil engineer here in a nothing little mining town like Harqua Hala?"

"Actually, the only impersonating I'm doing is the civilian part. I went to West Point, and every graduate of the Military Academy is technically an engineer until he chooses a branch of the Army for his regular duty.

"But to answer your question, Mr. Siringo," said Patton, "I'm here on a special assignment from the provost marshal. It concerns a top secret military project which I am not supposed to divulge to anyone. But since you gentlemen are men of great distinction and reputation, I think I would not be overstepping my authority by taking you into my confidence. Even so, I must ask each of you to give me your word that you will never reveal any of what I am about to tell you."

"You have it," said Earp.

"Also mine," said Siringo.

"Thank you, gentlemen." Patton paused, considering where to begin his tale. He started with a question. "Have either of you ever heard of phosgene?"

ELEVEN

A fine dust in the desert air over Arizona refracts the fading sunlight of evening, giving the land of a thousand canyons the most beautiful sunsets in the world.

Patton and Siringo sat on the porch of the Gold House after supper, enjoying just such a colorful twilight display. Siringo puffed on a cheroot, while Patton leaned back and relaxed in the cooling air as he contemplated everything Earp and Siringo had divulged to him that afternoon and as he second-guessed his own wisdom of revealing his purpose for being in Harqua Hala.

As they had walked, Earp recounted his conversation with Mamie Sattin in her room the night before. The details of the murder she imparted intrigued Siringo more than her disclosure that she had reason enough to kill Phillips. It didn't surprise the former Pinkerton that Phillips had jilted Mamie on more than one occasion even though she had been hopelessly in love with him since their first meeting nearly three decades before; Phillips always did have a reputation of being a ladies' man. But he was disappointed to learn that his old friend was responsible for Mamie's being a soiled dove. Mamie was an innocent young woman of eighteen when she met Phillips and immediately fell under his masculine spell. He left her a year later, unwed and in a family way, an outcast among her own people. The only friend she could find was Louisiana Sal Macomb, the manager of a local dance-hall troupe, who took her in and gave her a job as a seamstress. When Sal married and got out of the business, Mamie was left to fend for herself. The West being such a hard place, more so for women than for men, she had little other choice than to choose the world's oldest profession and give up her infant son for adoption.

Siringo presented a double revelation when it was his turn to talk.

Rising early that morning, he had ridden to Salome to telegraph Sheriff Farnsworth in Yuma, but when he found the telegrapher out of the office, he opted to employ the telephone and so placed a long-distance call to the lawman. He asked Farnsworth about Phillips having money, and the sheriff told him that he had found a bank deposit slip indicating that as of the first instant of the month prior to the murder Phillips had $4,926.32 in his account at the Harqua Hala Bank. Farnsworth had thought this unusual at the time of discovery but had done nothing toward that end during his investigation. When Siringo asked the sheriff about the mining claims Phillips owned, Farnsworth expressed ignorance and surprise that his deputy had been so well-off financially; Phillips certainly hadn't lived like a man of means. The next question was whether or not Phillips had any living relatives; Farnsworth could recall only one, an illegitimate son, of whom the sheriff knew nothing. Siringo then asked about a will; had Phillips left one? None was found. So who would get the money and the mining claims? The sheriff didn't have an answer.

Then Siringo told Earp and Patton about his visit to the bank and his discovery in the vault. This raised curious questions about Malcolm Caswell, the most important of which was whether there was a connection between Phillips having a fortune and the bank being short. The three men explored this possibility and came to the conclusion that further investigation was necessary before an answer could be found. It was decided that Farnsworth would have to make an official inquiry about Phillips' bank account. Patton would drive Siringo to Salome the next day to call Farnsworth and set the plan in motion.

The investigators came to the further conclusion that the illegitimate son Farnsworth had mentioned must have been the child Mamie Sattin had given up for adoption. It might have something to do with the murder; then again, it might be nothing at all. Earp argued the latter, but Siringo insisted that all possible leads should be followed until they proved out one way or the other. Earp agreed to question Mamie about it.

Their conversation then returned to Patton and his purpose for being in Harqua Hala.

The Army Ordnance Department had been experimenting in recent years with toxic gases as weapons of war and had been conducting some of these experiments at Fort Huachuca. Earlier in the year a single canister of chlorine gas, phosgene, vanished from the ordnance depot at the Arizona post. The provost marshal had absolutely no clues in the case until the murdered body of an enlisted man, the sergeant who had been in charge of the ammunition warehouse at the fort, was found in a hotel room in Phoenix. An investigation of the homicide led the provost marshal to the conclusion that the sergeant was involved in the disappearance of the phosgene canister and that he had accomplices, probably civilians. Interrogation of the hotel's personnel revealed the sergeant had been seen talking to another guest, a gentleman from Harqua Hala who had registered under the name of Benjamin Keenan. Patton was then chosen to go to Harqua Hala under the guise of a civil engineer working for the state of Arizona. His job was to find Keenan and learn everything he could about this man: who was he? who were his associates? what did he do? did he have the canister? and most important of all, what was he planning to do with the gas?

Thus far, Patton hadn't learned a thing. Since his arrival in the mining town, he had spent the time meeting people and carrying out his charade as a civil engineer.

Siringo offered to apply his detective expertise to Patton's problem, and by doing so, he prompted Earp to join in. The hotel clerk in Phoenix had described the sergeant's conversational partner as a gentleman dressed to the nines from his bowler to his polished boots. This meager description could fit only a few men in Harqua Hala. They listed them one by one—Malcolm Caswell, Ardmore Simpson, and Horace Beal—and just as quickly discarded each man as not having the look of a killer about him. But there was one man, Siringo noted; the man who had accompanied Simpson into the newspaper office the other day. Mr. Benteen. He was the only man they knew of to this point who fit the clerk's words, and Siringo noted that he did have the cold look of death about him. Earp suggested Patton pay a visit to the mining company's office and possibly meet Mr. Benteen. He would do that as soon as he and Siringo returned from Salome.

Patton continued to relax on the porch of the Gold House that evening, completely satisfied now that he had done the right thing by taking Earp and Siringo into his confidence. It was good to have two such distinguished men on his side; just their advice would prove invaluable, and already they had helped to build his self-esteem. As he allowed himself an indulgent smile of congratulations for this coup, his thoughts were interrupted by Siringo.

"George, I believe I'll wander down to the Dutchman's and play a little blackjack with Mr. Eagan before I turn in for the night," said Siringo. "Care to join me?"

"I've never played blackjack, Mr. Stewart," said Patton, continuing the charade of hidden identities although they were quite alone. "Poker is my game."

"It takes a cool head to be good poker player, and I can see by the look in your eye that you just might be pretty fair at the game. Am I right?"

Patton offered a modest smile and said, "I've turned an ace or two in my favor."

Siringo laughed and said, "Yes, I'll bet you have. Come along and I'll teach you the rudiments of the game . . . keep your losses at a minimum."

It was almost dark now, the full moon just then beginning to peek over the eastern horizon, as the two men stood and started across Gold Street. Patton walked toward Main Street, but Siringo directed his feet toward the alley that began just a few yards farther down Gold Street.

"If you don't mind, George," said Siringo, "I'd like to take the alley and have a look at the spot where that deputy sheriff was killed." There was no telling who might be within earshot, so Siringo had opted to refer to Walt Phillips by his position rather than by his name in order to make himself sound more like a casual curiosity seeker than a man with a direct interest in the murder case.

Playing along, Patton said, "Yes, let's go that way. I heard about that killing. Strange case, don't you think?"

Siringo frowned and said, "I really don't know too much about it myself."

Patton caught on to his own gaffe and said nothing more. He simply walked beside Siringo into the alley.

A minute later they passed the rear of the Dutchman's, then stopped behind Mrs. Gianelli's boardinghouse. The landlady's backyard was enclosed by a seven-foot wooden fence. It had a gate at the south corner, and beside it sat two old oil drums, now in use as trash barrels. Siringo walked over to the gate, turned, and looked back at the upper floor of the Dutchman's, Mamie Sattin's vantage point on the night of the murder. He nodded, as if in agreement with an unseen friend, then turned around to survey the area from there.

The jail was next door. All its windows were dark. The newspaper building was somewhat cater-cornered from there. Mr. Horace Beal must have been working late, for light could be seen through the curtained rear windows. There was a stable across the way and beyond that the mining company's machine shed. All dark in that direction.

Piano music and some occasional raucous laughter from the saloons disturbed the otherwise still night, but the distant din wasn't enough to drown out the opening and closing of Mrs. Gianelli's back door followed by the crunch of boots marching through the yard. Without delay, Siringo grabbed Patton by the arm and led him to and around the east corner of the fence. They heard the creak of the gate being opened and closed, then the footsteps moving away from them. Slowly, Siringo peeked around the corner of the fence and saw the ghostly form of a man walking rapidly toward the rear of the newspaper building.

He went to the back door and knocked. A moment later Horace Beal, wearing his work costume, opened the door and permitted his visitor entry. Then Beal did a curious thing. He stepped into the moonlit night and looked around, as if ascertaining whether someone had been watching. Evidently reassured that the new arrival had entered unseen, the newspaper publisher went back inside and closed the door.

"Something odd there," whispered Siringo.

"What's that?" asked Patton in a normal speaking voice.

"Talk softly, George," whispered Siringo. "There's no telling who's about in this dark."

"Okay," whispered Patton, "but what did you mean by 'odd'?"

"The way Beal looked around."

"So that's the Mr. Beal you were talking about this afternoon. You're right. He doesn't look like a killer."

"Not him, but who knows about the man who just went into Beal's office? I didn't see that much of him, but he was all spiffed up for a night on the town."

Before Patton could make a reply, another knock coming from the direction of the Harqua Hala *Miner* office reached their ears. Beal answered again, but this time his visitor was a petite woman.

Also again, Beal stepped outside and scanned the area before returning inside and closing the door.

"I'm beginning to think Mr. Beal has something to hide," whispered Siringo.

"It certainly looks that way," replied Patton softly.

"I think we might be wise to get a little closer and maybe hear what they're talking about in there."

It was a good idea but one foiled by the newspaper office door opening for the third time. Beal came outside wearing a coat and hat. The door closed behind him, obviously shut by one of the two visitors, and he walked straight up the alley toward Siringo and Patton.

The two spies inched away from the corner, hoping Beal would not come close enough to see them in the shadow of the Dutchman's. They waited, listening to Beal's footfalls come closer and closer. Then the publisher's rhythmic steps began to fade; he'd gone past their place of concealment. Cautiously, Siringo slipped into the alley and saw Beal heading straight toward the Gold House.

"Now if that don't beat all!" said Siringo in a normal voice. "Beal letting a young couple use his place for a secret rendezvous. I would have never guessed that in a million years, George. Would you?"

"No, never," said Patton.

"Well, I have no wish to be a Peeping Tom tonight. Let's go play some blackjack, George." He slapped Patton on the shoulder, and they headed for the street and the front door of the Dutchman's.

The bar was crowded with patrons—mostly businessmen and other non-miners, from the looks of their attire—and some of Mamie Sattin's ladies when Patton and Siringo entered the saloon, but the few gaming tables had open seats. Siringo guided his younger companion toward Earp's blackjack table, which was only half full. Earp was in the midst of a shuffle when they sat down.

"Good evening, Mr. Eagan," said Siringo. "How's your luck tonight?"

"Off and on, Mr. Stewart," replied Earp. "George, how are you this evening?"

"I'm looking to get a lesson in cards, Mr. Eagan," said Patton. "I just hope it's not too expensive."

"Minimum bet's a nickel, George," said Earp. "The limit's a C-note."

"A C-note?"

"Hundred dollars, George," said Siringo. "But don't worry about the limit right now. Wait till you've turned a few bucks before you start thinking about big bets."

Both men dug in their pockets, took out a few dollars in silver, and placed the coins on the table in front of them.

"Place your bets, gents," said Earp.

The other players—one, the day clerk from the Gold House; the second, a teller from the bank; and the other, the liveryman—accepted the invitation, each one placing a dime on his respective betting square. Siringo and Patton bet quarters.

Earp dealt the cards; both rounds face down. He turned up one of his cards: a queen.

The clerk stood pat; the teller, too. It was Patton's turn. He showed his cards—a six and a five—to Siringo.

"You permit doubling, Mr. Eagan?" asked Siringo.

"On any two cards," said Earp.

"Put another two bits out there, George." Patton did. "Now lay down your cards face up." Patton did that, too.

Earp took Patton's pasteboards, placed them in front of the bet, then slid a third card face down under the bet. He turned to Siringo.

"Mr. Stewart?"

"Give me a little one," said Siringo.

Earp flipped up a four and said, "Little enough?"

"Not bad. You always deal cards to order?"

The dealer didn't answer. He moved on to the next player. "Mr. Cartwright?"

The stable owner scratched a finger on the table, indicating he wanted a card. Earp obliged him, tossing out a king. Cartwright folded, throwing down a six and a seven.

Earp turned up his hole card, giving him sixteen. He took a hit, a five, making twenty-one.

"The name of the game, gents," said Earp. He checked the players' hands, raking in the bets of the losers and knocking the side of his hand on the table by Patton's bet to indicate they had pushed.

Before Earp could deal another round, Horace Beal came

through the back door, and the sweet lilt of children singing floated into the saloon. A hypnotic rapture smothered all activity in the Dutchman's. The room suddenly becoming very quiet, all the patrons and workers freezing in place, even conversations breaking off in midsentence. The song was "Amazing Grace," and the high pitch of the youthful singers lended accent to the Gaelic intonations of the tune, filling the night with conjured hauntings of Scottish castles and red-bearded, plaid-clad, kilted warriors wielding short swords and small round shields in the names of God, country, and clan.

The door closed, and the melody was muted. Several voices rose in a confused cacophony, but all demanded the same thing: "Open the door, fool!"

A previously preoccupied Beal was dumbfounded by the sudden outburst, but still he obeyed, almost instinctively, without delay.

The portal opened once again, the soft strains of the final verse dispelling the protestations and piercing the hearts of the listeners. And when the song was finished, all remained silent, almost reverent, until the next tune was begun. The more rapid rhythm of "Dixie" restored the partylike atmosphere of the saloon, instantly reviving some conversations but more often bringing on comment about the beauty of the lyrics and music and how much they meant to everyone.

"Suddenly," said Siringo, "I don't feel like playing cards. I think I'll go find those children and have myself a nice listen."

"I'll join you," said Patton.

They gathered up their money and headed for the back door, acknowledging and passing Beal along the way. Outside they went, turning instinctively toward the sound of the singing, then moving off in its direction.

Siringo and Patton found the children standing on the side of a small knoll just east of Gold Street near the stamp mill. The group was made up of twenty or so school-age youngsters and a few of their mothers. Another woman, presumably also a parent, directed the makeshift choir. Other folks had gathered in small knots along the road to listen to the seemingly impromptu concert.

Two more songs—"Oh, Susanna," with a twist whereby Arizona was substituted for Alabama, and "The Battle Hymn of the Republic"—were sung. Then during a momentary pause Siringo remarked, "Something odd here, George. See that lad on the hill?"

"Up there on top?"

"That's the one. Keep an eye on him and an ear to the beginning of the next song. Watch what he does."

The boy in question stood facing the other side of the knoll. He held a large neckerchief in one hand at his side. A minute passed, then he turned toward the director of the singers and wiped his face rather casually.

Instantly, the song leader raised her hands, called out the name of the next tune—"America, the Beautiful"—and the chorus began to sing.

"Did you see that, George?" asked Siringo, still watching the youngster on the hill.

"Yes, I did," said Patton. "It was like he was signaling the choirmistress to—"

"Precisely, George. He was signaling her to begin the next song. The question is why."

The children were only half into the first verse when Siringo got an answer.

Ardmore Simpson, followed by several armed men, including Mr. Benteen, came marching down the street from the offices of the Harqua Hala Mining Company. It was easy to see by the way they walked that they were cold, determined men bent on mayhem.

"What do you make of this?" asked Patton.

"Trouble," said Siringo.

The boy on the knoll had disappeared, and the other children had stopped singing. The lady leading the singers called one of the bigger lads over to her, said something to him quickly, then sent him running off toward the business district. Other women rounded up the remaining youngsters and began herding them away from the scene toward their homes in Ditch Town. Most of the onlookers held their ground, but a few did disperse, seemingly in panic.

Simpson divided his force, sending half to the top of the knoll with Mr. Benteen at their head, while he led the others around the hill to the south.

"Whatever is to happen," said Siringo, "will happen on the other side of the rise. Care to get a closer look, George?"

"I'm game."

They headed up the hill after Benteen's bunch, and others followed their lead. Halting at the crest, they had a perfect view of the scene unfolding on the other side in the bright moonlight.

More than a score of miners with picks and shovels scurried over the arrastra beds below, some carrying buckets filled with their evening's work, scrapings of residual gold from the smelter slag. Simpson and Benteen had spread their men into two assault lines, rifles and revolvers ready for action if necessary, flanking the miners to the north and south. The hill lay to the west and a deep ravine to the east. Seeing that their paths of escape were blocked, the miners formed up in two semicircular defense perimeters, facing the opposition.

"All right, you thieves!" shouted Simpson. "Just hold it right there, and don't anyone move! These men have orders to shoot anyone who tries to run."

The miners tightened their lines, backing up until they were shoulder to shoulder and back to back. Each man held a tool in front of him, prepared to defend his life.

"There is no need for anyone to get hurt here," said Simpson, "as long as you do as you're told. Just put down those picks and shovels, and if any of you have guns, you can throw them out where we can see them."

A silence followed as none of the miners moved or threw down his weapon.

"Mexican standoff," said Siringo softly.

Simpson appeared to be miffed about what to do next.

But not Benteen. He cocked the hammer of his .44 and leveled it at the miner closest to him. The men with him did likewise.

"Mr. Simpson!" he shouted. "I believe I see a man who wants to run off with some of your gold."

"Then you know what to do, Mr. Benteen."

"Hold on there, gunfighter!"

The command came from a newcomer to the scene; the same man Siringo and Patton had seen earlier going into the Harqua Hala *Miner.* He topped the hill several yards to the right of them; Horace Beal trailing a few paces behind him.

Benteen swung around and took aim at the new arrival.

"Friedkin!" shouted Simpson in disgust. "I should have known you'd be here, you damn Bolshevik!"

"That's right, Mr. Simpson," answered Friedkin. "I am here . . . to stop you and your thugs from murdering these good men."

"These thieves, you mean!" retorted Simpson.

"They are only collecting what you have thrown away."

"This is my land, and these are my arrastra beds. And whatever gold there is in them belongs to me."

"Ill-gotten gain!" interjected Beal, now beside Friedkin at the bottom of the hill between the miners and Simpson's group.

"You stay out of this, Beal," said the mine owner, "or Mr. Benteen might mistake you for one of these thieving miners."

Earp and Deputy Sheriff Jake Poole suddenly appeared beside Siringo and Patton.

"What gives here?" asked Earp.

"It appears we have the makings of a war," said Siringo.

"This isn't your land, Simpson," said Friedkin. "This property belongs to the Triple H Land Company, and you have no rights here."

"The Triple H Land Company?" echoed Simpson. "Who in Hades is that?"

Beal reached out and stopped Friedkin from offering an answer, whispering something into the taller, younger man's ear. Friedkin nodded, then turned his attention back to Simpson.

"Never mind that, Simpson," said Friedkin. "The point is, you and your thugs are breaking the law."

"We're breaking the law? You're the ones breaking the law here."

"No, sir, we are not!" shouted Friedkin. "You are trespassing here! Now leave or—"

Beal again interrupted Friedkin with a tug at his arm and a whisper.

"I don't like the looks of this," said Earp. "Deputy, you'd better do something to stop this from becoming a fight."

"Not me," said Poole. "I'm not going up against Simpson and his hired guns."

"You're the law here, Poole!" snapped Earp. "Do your duty!"

"What duty? No one's made any complaint to me, and so far as I can see, no one's broken any laws yet."

Earp grabbed Poole's elbow and growled, "It's your job to keep the peace, Deputy, and if you don't do your job, I'll be obliged to let my good and old friend Sheriff C. H. Farnsworth know about it."

"You know Sheriff Farnsworth?"

"For thirty years," said Earp.

"But . . . Mr. Eagan . . . Benteen is a killer."

Earp looked into Poole's eyes and saw the fear in them. He felt a twinge in his heart; sympathy at first, then the wizened understanding of age. In spite of his braggadocio and cocky ways, Poole had never used his gun. Earp turned to Siringo to ask a singular question, but a knowing nod from the former Pinkerton's man answered him before he could speak the words. He looked at Patton.

"George, have you got your shoulder piece?" asked Earp.

Patton touched his left breast and said, "Loaded and ready."

"We'll back your play, Deputy," said Earp. "Just swear us in, and we'll put a halt to this now before someone gets killed."

Poole looked from one man to the next, then said, "Okay, you're sworn in." He hitched up his gun belt and started down the hill toward Simpson.

Earp, Patton, and Siringo walked a pace behind Poole until they reached the bottom of the hill, where they fanned out and moved up alongside him. Earp felt a flickering flash of déjà vu, and a rush of ice steeled his nerve. As the foursome approached the mine owner, the three newly sworn deputies discreetly produced their guns, each holding his at his side.

Seeing Poole and the deputized cohort move down the hill toward his employer, Benteen lowered his Colt somewhat, cautioned his men to hold their ground, then hurried to join Simpson.

The miners facing Benteen's group had already turned to watch their champion confront their antagonist, but they remained in place, knowing full well that Simpson's hired guns might open up on them at the slightest provocation.

Nearly everyone in town had now gathered on the hill like so many lords and ladies at a medieval joust, each in support of one side or the other, but all hoping for some excitement to break the usual boredom of the desert West.

Spying the approaching lawmen, Simpson and Friedkin broke off their argument and waited. Benteen gave the foursome a wide berth as he passed them. The deputies halted in front of Simpson just as Benteen took up a firm position beside his boss. The gunman still had his revolver ready, though lower now. Simpson noted the level of his man's weapon and gently put a hand on Benteen's arm, pushing it downward until the shootist understood that he was to rest the .44 at his side.

The night, already heavy with tension and anticipation, suddenly became darker as a cloud passed in front of the moon; an ominous omen at best. Nothing stirred as both spectators and participants held a collective breath. As the silvery lunar light reappeared, Earp nudged Poole into action.

"Mr. Simpson, uh," stammered Poole, "it's my . . . uh . . . duty to order you to disperse your men and leave these peaceable citizens go their way."

"You what?" Simpson was all abluster. "You, Poole? You're giving me orders?" He elbowed Benteen. "Is that rich or what, eh, Benteen? This sniveling pup is giving me orders." He feigned a mocking laugh, then became deadly serious again. "Out of the way, Poole. This is no concern of yours."

"I am sworn to keep the peace in this town, Mr. Simpson," said the deputy, suddenly finding new strength in his character, fed by a rising anger precipitated by Simpson's disparaging, insulting attitude. "The way I see it, you're trying to incite a riot here, and that means you're disturbing the peace. I will give you just one minute to leave this area and take your men with you or—"

Benteen interrupted the threat. "Or what, Poole?"

Hearing Benteen's low, guttural tone struck an old note in Siringo's memory. He knew this man now.

"Or," said Poole slowly, "my deputies and I will arrest you for inciting a riot and disturbing the peace."

Benteen started to raise his gun, but Simpson stayed his hand, saying, "I'll handle this." His stare never left Poole's face. "You try to arrest me, Poole, and these men will stop you and your deputies quite dead."

Finally getting his fill of this pompous ass and recalling a similar incident of years before in Tombstone, Earp said, "Maybe so, sir, but there are four of us. And before your men can kill all four of us, one of us will kill you. I promise you that."

Simpson was unnerved. Even in the moonlight, he could see that the grit in Earp's steely blue eyes was more than brass. He flinched, marking himself as a dead man should lead fly. And he knew it.

"Okay, Poole," said Simpson, speaking to the younger man in an attempt to insult Earp by ignoring him, "we'll go . . . straight to your office, where I will swear out a complaint against Friedkin and these men for stealing my gold."

"Don't bother," said Poole. "If what Mr. Friedkin says about this land not being yours is true, then you have no complaint."

"What? Do you mean to do nothing about this?"

"I've done all I'm going to do unless you don't leave here pronto. When and if you can prove this land is yours, I will personally arrest each and every one of these men, starting with Mr. Friedkin. And I promise you that."

Shaking his head in disgust, Simpson said, "Okay, Poole. We'll do it your way . . . for now. Put your gun away, Benteen, and let's get out of here. I'll deal with these thieves later."

Benteen did as ordered, and so did the rest of the gunmen. Then all of them followed Simpson back toward the mining company's offices.

A cheer went up from the miners as they surrounded the deputies to thank them for saving them from Benteen and his henchmen. Friedkin was the first to offer to shake Poole's hand, but the lawman disdained the congratulatory gesture.

"You're a troublemaker, Friedkin," said Poole, "and I don't like troublemakers. You incite these people to do something stupid like this once more, and I won't stop Simpson until it's too late. You get my drift, Friedkin?"

Friedkin smiled knowingly and nodded.

Poole addressed the miners and the spectators. "Now you people go back to your homes. It's all over. No one's been hurt, and I don't want to see something like this again. Now go home!"

There were grumblings among the miners, and some were ready to offer argument. Friedkin stopped any further disturbance.

"Mr. Poole is right, men. Let's all go home and get a good night's rest. There's still plenty of work to be done."

The miners dispersed, taking their tools and buckets of arrastra scrapings with them. Friedkin and Beal headed back to town and Beal's office. All onlookers except one also departed. The last straggler, a very old man, approached the deputies.

"How'd you do?" said the old man, extending a withered hand to Earp. "Lester T. Higgins is the name. Been here since the start.

Ain't seen nothing like this before. Not here, anyways. But I saw something like it happen back in Tombstone years ago. Wyatt Earp, it was. Held off a lynch mob all by hisself. Just like you did with Simpson, he told the leader of the mob he'd be the first one to die if they didn't break off and go home. And just like Simpson did, he went home, too. Yep, that was some sight. Just like Wyatt Earp in the old days."

TWELVE

"Quite a stir tonight," said Mamie Sattin as she poured liquor into three shot glasses. "That's the closest they've come to killing each other so far."

"Who's that?" asked Earp.

"The miners and Simpson's hired guns." She recapped the bottle, picked up two of the drinks, and gave one each to her guests. "They've all been building up for a big blow for more than a month now. It started getting serious just about the time Walt was killed." She got her own drink and sat down.

"What's it all about, Mamie?" asked Siringo.

"Money. Or the lack of it." She downed the slug of booze before continuing. "The gold is paying out in the mine. Has been for more than a year. That's why Simpson hired Friedkin. He knows there's more gold in that mountain, but he doesn't know where. So instead of having the miners dig a whole bunch of new shafts all over the place, he hired Friedkin to blast holes in it in hopes he'd uncover a new vein."

"Has he had any luck yet?" asked Earp.

"A little," said Mamie. "They found a couple of pockets that assayed out pretty good, but that's all they were. Only pockets. In the meantime, the gold in the main mine keeps getting thinner and thinner."

"So why are the miners agitating?" asked Siringo. "If the gold is paying out and they know it, why don't they just pull up stakes and move on? That's what sensible folks in most dying mining camps do."

"Simpson isn't the only one who's convinced there's more gold in that mountain. Friedkin has the miners believing it, too. He's been telling them through speeches and articles in the paper that Simpson knows there's more gold in the mountain but that he doesn't want to mine it because he would have to share it with the miners."

"How's that?" asked Earp.

"Most of these people have been here for several years," said Mamie. "Harqua Hala will be twenty years old next year. The first five years were the best. The gold was coming out of the mountain real easy, and the mining company was shipping as much as four hundred pounds a week out of here."

Siringo let out a low whistle to show his appreciation of what that meant in dollars and cents, then said, "That's almost a half million a year. Must have been a rich vein."

"It was," said Mamie. "Then I understand it split, then each runner split. This called for more men to mine the gold, and paying more men meant less profit. The mining company began changing owners about as regular as most folks take a bath. Then Simpson bought it three years back. Like all the others, he put some new life in the town when he got here, and things were better for a while. Then Simpson found out what it was costing him to mind the gold. He fired every fifth miner last year, but then the rest of them quit in protest. So he hired them all back and lowered their wages. The miners didn't like that, so they quit on him again. So he came up with the old idea of paying each man according to how much gold he dug out of the mountain. The miners liked that idea until Friedkin showed up last winter. He quickly pointed out that the miners were working harder but weren't making any more money for it. Simpson fired Friedkin right off, but the miners quit until he was rehired. That was just a few weeks before Walt was killed."

"Mamie, this fellow Benteen," said Siringo. "How much do you know about him?"

"Not much. Simpson doesn't talk about him. He came here just about the time Simpson fired Friedkin. Maybe a week before. He doesn't come into the Dutchman's very often. Sticks to the mining company's property mostly. I'll tell you one thing, though. You never see him in town without Simpson. Same with Simpson. He never leaves his house without Benteen. I think the only time Benteen ain't with him is when he's up here."

"This business over the arrastra beds," said Earp. "How long has that been going on?"

"The miners have been going out there once a week for the last month or so. This is the first time Simpson's done anything about it. It's funny, you know. I knew he had a few more men besides

Benteen, but I didn't know he had that many hired guns around. I wonder where they've been hiding all this time."

"What do you mean by that?" asked Earp.

"I've seen every one of them before. Two, three times at least. But this is the first time I've seen them all at once. What's more, I didn't know they worked for Simpson."

"I don't think I understand," said Earp.

"Well, Wyatt, they've been in the Dutchman's, a couple, three of them at a time. They show up in town, tie one on for a few days, then they disappear again."

"How long has this been going on?" asked Siringo.

"About four or five months."

"Got any idea where they come from or where they go?" asked Siringo.

"Nope. They come to town filthy as miners after a month in the hole, get themselves drunk, go down to the tonsorial parlor and get cleaned up, then come here and visit my ladies. Next morning they're gone. They always come in groups of three or four about two weeks apart."

"Were any of them in town the night Walt Phillips was killed?" asked Siringo.

"No, I don't think so."

"I'm still curious about your earlier remark," said Earp, "when you said you wondered where these men have been hiding."

"Yes," said Siringo, "I've been wondering about that myself. Simpson must have had twenty guns out there tonight. And you say only a few of them stay here in town all the time?"

"That's right," said Mamie. "There's Benteen and three others who guard the place day and night. When there's a gold shipment, two of them ride shotgun on the wagon to Salome."

"And the rest only come into town occasionally?" asked Earp.

"That's right."

"You know, Charlie, we might be wise to find out where these fellows are staying."

"And," said Siringo, "find out what they do when they aren't here in town. That remark about how they look like miners after they've been in the hole for a month has piqued my curiosity as well."

"Are you thinking Simpson might have another mining operation going somewhere else?" asked Earp. "An illegal operation that maybe Walt Phillips found out about?"

"It's possible," said Siringo. "But we'll need proof."

"Then we'd better get it," said Earp.

"Mamie," said Siringo, "there's something else I found curious tonight. Before all the ruckus at the arrastra beds, George and I were out back of here, taking a look at the spot where Walt was killed, and we saw Friedkin and a young lady go into the newspaper building."

"Oh, that. Friedkin and Charlotte Simpson have been sneaking in there a couple nights a week ever since he came to town. I guess I don't have to tell you why they have to do that."

"No, I think we can figure that out," said Siringo. "What I don't understand is how Beal is involved."

"Like I told Wyatt, Beal has been on the side of the miners ever since the trouble started. He's done as much to stir them up as Friedkin has. He's always spouting off that Simpson exploits the miners, takes advantage of their ignorance, and forces them to work for slave wages just so they can barely feed their families."

"So Friedkin and Beal are pretty thick," said Siringo. "That is interesting."

"And Simpson's daughter is seeing Friedkin on the sly," said Earp. "I wonder how that got started. Mamie, didn't you say that Simpson's daughter had to leave some eastern girls' school because of trouble with a man?"

"That's right, I did," said Mamie. "And she came here just before Friedkin showed up. You don't think—"

"Yes, I do," said Earp. "Charlie, you got any idea on how we can find out for sure that Friedkin and Simpson's daughter might have known each other back East?"

"We do have an old friend in New York," said Siringo. "Maybe a telegram to him might get us the information we want."

"My thinking exactly," said Earp.

"There's something else that might interest you," said Mamie, "now that you seem to be interested in Charlotte Simpson and Friedkin."

"What's that, Mamie?" asked Earp.

"While she's been seeing Friedkin on the sly at night, Jake Poole has been pursuing her in the daytime."

"Pursuing, Mamie?" queried Siringo. "That's an odd term for courtship."

"It ain't exactly courtship, Charlie," said Mamie. "Jake's been head over heels for that girl since she first arrived here. He follows her around like a lovesick puppy. The way he practically foams at the mouth whenever she's in sight is downright disgusting. The worst part of it is Jake thinks that girl is in love with him, too. A couple of months back he let it be known that he and she were going to be hitched. When Little Miss High-and-mighty heard about that, she went storming all around town looking for Jake to give him what-for. Only Jake was gone to Salome that day. She had the whole town buzzing. Then Walt got killed, and folks had something else to talk about."

THIRTEEN

Simpson's private office was actually in his home atop the "Bosom" closest to the business district of Harqua Hala. From the front stoop of the two-story adobe and Spanish tile structure, the view took in the whole town, but one could only see the mining area from the window of Simpson's sanctuary.

Patton stared through the glass and pretended to be intrigued by the activity around the stamp mill as he waited for Simpson to join him. The bandage on his right hand reminded him of the events of the day before.

After an early breakfast of *huevos rancheros con carne y tortillas*, Patton drove Siringo over the hills to the train depot at Salome. The nine-mile trip took them a little more than half an hour.

Salome wasn't much more than a water stop for the Atchison, Topeka & Santa Fe Railroad line that ran from Wickenburg to Parker on the Colorado River and from there across the vast Mohave Desert to the fertile valleys of southern California. The town consisted of Sheffler's Hotel and Saloon, a general store, a few houses made of adobe, a few more made of wood, the depot, and the stockyards. An east-west road was the major thoroughfare; the only other street being the two-track south to Harqua Hala. A windmill pumped water from a deep well for the railroad's tank, which also served the town.

The railroad had installed Salome's only telephone as a quicker and cheaper method of communicating with the company agent there, but as time passed and others in town began using it to call Wickenburg or Phoenix or Yuma, the stationmaster started charging for its use. When Siringo asked to call Sheriff Farnsworth, the cost was two bits.

"Clyde? Charlie Siringo here."

"Charlie, how are you? I didn't expect to hear from you again for a while. I haven't even had a chance to find out who owns the Triple H Land Company. But maybe you've already found Walt's killer."

"We're getting closer, Clyde, but before I can pin him down, I need some more information and some help."

"Anything I can do to help," said Farnsworth.

"You can start by finding out what ever happened to Ben Kilpatrick."

"Ben Kilpatrick? The killer that rode with Butch Cassidy and the Sundance Kid?"

"The same. I think he's presently residing in Harqua Hala."

"You think? Don't you know for sure? I mean—"

"It's been years since I pulled that little trick on Cassidy's Hole-in-the-Wall Gang. A man's looks change with time, and besides, Kilpatrick didn't spend that much time at the hideout back then. He was too busy sparking Laura Bullion."

"Now there's a name I haven't heard in years," said the sheriff. "Seems to me I heard that Kilpatrick bought it one night at her place in Evanston, Wyoming."

"Not true," said Siringo. "I started that rumor myself to scare Cassidy and Longbaugh into giving themselves up. Instead, they ran off to South America. I lost track of all of them after that. I did hear that Harvey Logan started up a gang, but that bunch didn't get too far. I don't think Kilpatrick was with them. Logan wasn't his type of leader."

"What's the name of this man that you suspect might be Kilpatrick?"

"Benteen," said Siringo. Then eyeing Patton, he added, "Might also be Benjamin Keenan."

"Neither one of those rings any bells, Charlie, but I'll check on both and see what I can come up with."

"Now there's this other thing about Walt's money," said Siringo. "I need someone to make a claim on it at the bank in Harqua Hala."

"Whatever for?" asked Farnsworth.

"I paid the bank a visit and found out Mr. Caswell, the banker, isn't too certain about how much money he has in his vault."

"You think the bank might be short?"

"Could be. That's why I want you or someone to lay claim to

Walt's money. If Mr. Caswell can't come up with it on demand, then you might want to take an official look at him and his books."

"I'm not following you, Charlie. What's this got to do with Walt's murder?"

"I could be wrong about this fellow Benteen being mixed up in it. For all I know at this point, Walt might have found out about a shortage at the bank, and Caswell killed him to shut him up. Or maybe Caswell knew Walt didn't have any living relatives, and with the shortage, maybe he figured he could make it up by doing in Walt. Could be some other reason, or maybe I'm barking up the wrong tree. It's just that I have to follow up all possibilities."

"Well, I'm not sure what I can do, Charlie, but if it'll help find Walt's killer, then I'll do it. When I get something, how do I let you know about it?"

"Letter would be too slow. Telegram might be a problem. I'm not too sure we can trust anyone here. We could drive over here every day and check with you on the telephone."

"We? Is Earp with you?"

"No," said Siringo. "Uh, he's probably still sleeping back in Harqua Hala."

"Then who's with you? Who drove you to Salome?"

Siringo hesitated to answer, thinking that he may have made a mistake. To this point, Farnsworth had been unaware of Patton, and to mention the Army officer now might compromise him. The former Pinkerton glanced sheepishly at Patton, then returned his attention to the sheriff.

"Clyde, Wyatt and I took another man into our confidence."

"Another man? Who?"

"His name is George . . . Patterson. Young fellow. Son of an old friend of Wyatt's and mine from Alaska."

"What's he doing in Harqua Hala?" asked Farnsworth.

"He went to California to look up Wyatt, and Wyatt's wife told him where he could find Wyatt. George has an automobile, so he drove me over here this morning."

"Well, if he's all right with you and Wyatt, then I guess it's okay."

"Of course George is okay," said Siringo. "Now like I was saying, we could drive over here every day and call you, but that might make someone suspicious. We could come over every other day or so. That way we could avert suspicion for a while."

"Well, let's hope it doesn't take too long," said the sheriff. "Roosevelt is coming to Arizona to campaign next week, and I understand his train will be stopping in Salome and Parker on his way to California. If he does stop in my county, I'll have to put on some extra deputies and come up there to guard him, then ride the train to Parker to do it again."

"Roosevelt you say? Well, that should make Mr. Beal happy. Give him some real news for his paper."

Farnsworth chuckled on the other end of the line, then said, "So you've met Mr. Horace Beal, I take it. A real firebrand, that one. When Roosevelt was President before, Beal was always praising him for helping the workingman. But when Taft started running the country downhill, Beal blamed Roosevelt for picking Taft. When I was up there last month looking into Walt's murder, I noticed a copy of Beal's paper in Walt's office where Beal had written an editorial on the three candidates. He was backing Wilson. So with Roosevelt coming here now, I suppose he'll be writing another one of those scathing editorials. Makes no difference to me. No matter which one gets elected, he won't change nothing for Arizona."

"I'm not much on politics," said Siringo. "I'll call you again in a couple of days."

They broke the connection.

"George," said Siringo, "the ride over here made me a little thirsty. What do you say to getting a drink at the saloon before we head back?"

"Sounds good to me," said Patton.

Sheffler's Hotel and Saloon was down the road and across the tracks from the depot. Patton drove them there.

The bar had only one customer. A grizzled old prospector stood at the rail, nursing a mug of foamy beer. The beverage looked good to Siringo and Patton, so they ordered the same. Siringo was in a beneficent mood, so he told the bartender to draw another brew for the gold hunter.

"Well, thank you, stranger," said the prospector, raising his glass in salute to his benefactor. He took a long swallow, then slid down the bar to join the newcomers. "Al Ziegler is my name. A to Z, that's me. Prospector. Been looking for gold in these mountains most of the summer. I scouted the Bradshaws last year, but I guess most of the gold in those hills has been found. Fact is, I've prospected most of the higher ranges in this territory. Just now getting around to the desert areas. Who might you two fellows be?"

"Clayton Stewart is my name," said Siringo, "and my young friend here is George Patton. I'm in the cattle business, and Mr. Patton is a civil engineer. We're staying at the Gold House in Harqua Hala."

"What brings you this way?" asked Ziegler.

"Came over to use the telephone at the train depot," said Siringo.

"Telephone you say? I've seen them, but I've never had the occasion to use one. I've seen electric lights, too. Heard a phonograph once. But I ain't seen none of them new moving-picture shows yet. Don't get into big towns much. Too many people. Don't like being crowded. That's why I prospect. I find me a little gold here and there. Enough to get me another grubstake and keep me going.

"No-sir-ree! Don't like being crowded. It's getting so you can't even walk the desert anymore without running into someone. Take yesterday, for instance. There I was, minding my own business, just me and Cordelia walking along the railroad. Cordelia, that's my burro. Been with me four years now. Had an ornery mule named Harold before that. Had to shoot him. Broke a leg. Sure ate good for a whole month that winter.

"Anyways, like I was saying, Cordelia and me was walking along the railroad tracks, minding our own business, when all of a sudden some fellow jumps up from behind a rock up on the side of a hill and takes a potshot at me. Scared the bejeebers out of Cordelia . . . and me, too. We scrambled down the grade into a wash just as another shot went whizzing over our heads. Well, we skedaddled down that wash and got ourselves the heck out of there. Don't know why that fellow was shooting at us, but I'll tell you this. I won't be taking no more shortcuts through no more railroad tunnels when I want to get somewheres in a hurry."

"Did you report this to the law?" asked Patton.

"What law?" queried Ziegler. "You see any sheriffs or marshals around here?"

"There's a deputy in Harqua Hala," said Patton.

"He ain't here, though," said Ziegler, "and I ain't going to Harqua Hala. I already heard the gold's payed out in those hills. Fellow over to Quartzsite told me that. We was talking about prospecting because he had the look of a prospector . . . or a miner. Said he wasn't neither when I asked him. But I ought to know another gold hunter when I see one. Been doing it long enough. I should know. Fellow was dirty enough for two or three good men who been down in a hole for a month."

"What's that you say, Mr. Ziegler?" asked Siringo, his curiosity finally aroused.

"You hard of hearing, Mr. Stewart? Or weren't you listening? I was telling you how I was shot at yesterday."

"Yes, I know, Mr. Ziegler," said Siringo impatiently. "I was inquiring about the dirty gentleman to whom you spoke in Quartzsite. Did I hear you correctly when you said he 'was dirty enough for two or three good men'?"

"That's exactly what I said, Mr. Stewart. He was downright filthy. Smelled bad, too."

"And he was in Quartzsite?"

"That's right. Quartzsite. That's about—"

"I'm familiar with the town, Mr. Ziegler," said Siringo, cutting the prospector short. "This man, did he have a name?"

"Course he did," said Ziegler. "But I didn't catch it. He wasn't exactly one of your friendly types, if you know what I mean. Not like you two fellows. We talked for ten, fifteen minutes, and he never once offered to buy me a drink."

Siringo noted that Ziegler's glass was empty and promptly took his cue. He ordered another round.

"Right nice of you, Mr. Stewart," said Ziegler, again raising his mug in salute.

"You're quite welcome, Mr. Ziegler. Please tell me more about this man you met in Quartzsite."

"Why?" asked Ziegler. Then he belched.

"I'm something of an amateur sleuth, Mr. Ziegler. Sort of a Sherlock Holmes of the sage, you might say."

"Sherlock who?"

"Holmes," said Siringo. "He's a fictional detective who solves various crimes on the skimpiest clues. He has great powers of observation and deduction. I like to think that I am just as good a man, so I practice these traits as a hobby."

Ziegler stared at him in disbelief. Then he said, "I ain't exactly sure about what you're saying there, Mr. Stewart, but as long as you're buying, I guess I'll tell you whatever you want to hear."

"Just the facts, Mr. Ziegler. Please stick to the facts."

"Okay, I'll do my best." Ziegler took another long pull on the beer, leaving the glass nearly empty. "As I was saying, this fellow denied being a prospector or a miner, but I knew he was lying. He was just too dirty not to be. Well, sir, that got me to thinking that just maybe he was lying because he had something to hide. Like a new strike, maybe. So I thought I'd hang around Quartzsite till he left, and then I'd follow him."

"Was he alone in Quartzsite?" asked Siringo.

"Nope. There was another fellow with him. Just as dirty as he was when I first saw him, but I didn't get to talk to him. He come into the saloon, had one quick beer, then skedaddled himself to the barber for a bath and a shave and haircut. When he came back, the fellow I was talking to took his turn. Wouldn't have known him if he hadn't sidled up to his compadre in the saloon and told him to go get himself a bath."

"When was this, Mr. Ziegler?" asked Siringo. "I mean, what day was it?"

Ziegler emptied his glass and set it down for the bartender to refill.

"Four days back," said Ziegler. "Next day, they was gone. Didn't see them leave town, but the bartender at the saloon told me those two were the last of a whole bunch that came into town two days before and that the rest of them had pulled out just before I got there."

"You don't say?"

"I do," said Ziegler. "A whole bunch of them dirty fellows. Then the two I saw. Got me to thinking that they was from some mining camp I hadn't heard about, so I let it go and headed out this way. Followed the main road through the mountains, then across the valley till I met up with the railroad at Hope. That's when I figured it would be easier to go through the tunnel instead of winding my way through Granite Pass. Besides, I could get out of the hot sun for a while.

"Well, I wasn't but a hundred yards or so from the tunnel entrance when the first shot kicked up dust at my feet. That's when Cordelia and me decided the sun wasn't so hot that day."

"That's all very interesting, Mr. Ziegler. I thank you for sharing your tale with us." Siringo fished into his vest pocket for a silver dollar, found one, and placed it on the counter. "Barkeeper, see that Mr. Ziegler's glass doesn't run dry as long as he's thirsty."

"Thank you, Mr. Stewart. That's right nice of you."

Siringo and Patton left Sheffler's for the Hupmobile.

"George, how do you feel about a little adventure?"

"What have you got in mind, Charlie?"

"Has this thing got enough fuel in it for a drive out to Granite Pass?"

"More than enough."

The Harqua Hala and Harcuvar Mountains grew out of the desert floor in the shape of a horseshoe, with the Harqua Halas forming the southern arm and the Harcuvars the northern wing. Granite Pass was the natural cut between the two ranges and lay west-southwest of Salome, a distance of six miles. The valley rose gently to the jigsaw pass, narrowing to the precise point where it started its downward course into the Bouse Valley.

The road to Granite Pass paralleled the Atchison, Topeka & Santa Fe Railroad tracks for the first few miles until the railway veered off on a more westerly course. A knoll split the two routes for another mile before they came close together again in the pass, the steel highway running along the north side of the ravine slashing its way into the next valley and the dirt and gravel track winding down the south side. Halfway through Granite Pass, a finger of the Harcuvars gouged into the cut, causing the road to make a wide curve, but forcing the railway to bore through the mountain.

As the Hupmobile came within sight of the tunnel, Siringo motioned for Patton to halt the vehicle, forgoing words that would have been useless against the noise of the engine echoing off the canyon walls. Patton accepted the direction, stopped the car at the side of the road, and shut down the motor.

"Mr. Ziegler said he was coming from Quartzsite when he approached the tunnel," said Siringo, "and the gunman fired at him from the hill above the tunnel. Quartzsite lies yonder." He pointed to the west. "I wonder if that bushwhacker is still around up there."

"I don't see anyone up there," said Patton.

"He could be in hiding, watching us right now. Maybe as long as we stay here on the road and don't go snooping around the tunnel he won't bother us. Then again, maybe he's only watching the other side of the hill. What's your guess, George?"

"We were taught at the Academy not to go up against an enemy until we knew that enemy's strength of force," said Patton, now the military man. "Guessing might get us killed, Charlie. I think a little reconnaissance is called for here."

Siringo peered quizzically at the young Army officer and said, "A little re-what?"

"Reconnaissance," said Patton, as if repeating the term would explain its meaning. Seeing Siringo's expression, he said, "Reconnoiter . . . survey the enemy position for the purpose—"

"Yes, of course," said Siringo, suddenly understanding. "A scouting expedition. Yes, of course, we should scout their position. Precisely my thought, George. How would you have us go about it?"

"No offense, Charlie, but I was thinking I should do it . . . alone. I mean—"

"I know what you mean, George. You think I'm too old to be climbing around these hills like a mountain goat, don't you? Well, you could be right, but if I let you go alone and that bushwhacker is up there and he puts a slug in you, what happens to me then? How would I get back to Salome? I don't know how to drive this contraption of yours, and as *old* as I am, I'd die from thirst before I could walk back. No, George. When Wyatt and I took you into our confidence, we became partners, and that means we share everything equally . . . including the danger."

"I didn't mean anything by—"

"I know you didn't, George, and I appreciate your concern for my well-being. But we've got us a job to do, so let's do it. If it'll make you feel any better, I'll take the low ridge and you can take the higher one."

"Sounds good to me, Charlie," said Patton with a smile.

"Just remember, George. This is a scouting trip, not a battle. We're just going up there to see what we can see."

"Understood. We look around and meet back here, right?"

Siringo winked at him and said, "That's the ticket."

They got out of the car and walked to the edge of the ravine. Siringo opened his coat, took his piece—a Colt Pocket .41—from its holster on his hip, checked the cylinder for bullets, then replaced it. Patton did likewise with his weapon—a short-barreled Smith & Wesson Pocket .38.

"Remember what Teddy Roosevelt once said about being hard?" said Siringo.

"You mean 'Walk softly and carry a big stick'?"

"Exactly, George. Be as quiet as you can. Keep off the loose rocks and don't start any slides. If you see anyone up there, keep low and watch and listen."

"What if whoever might be up there sees me first and decides to take a shot at me like he did at the old prospector?"

"Then let's hope his aim is still bad, George."

Patton stared at Siringo and said, "Yeah, sure."

They started down into the ravine, each being careful not to make any noise. In another minute, they climbed up the other side to the railroad tracks. Patton crossed the rails and headed up the mountainside. Siringo began walking toward the tunnel.

It took Patton a quarter of an hour to reach the top of the first hill; Siringo was out of sight. He followed the crest's upward trail as it snaked in the general direction of the ridge over the railroad tunnel. An outcropping of sunburned granite blocked his path. Patton had only one precarious choice around it. He skirted the crumbling rocks on the shady side, hugging the vertical stone face tightly as best as he could with each step.

A rifle shot rang out, echoing through the hills.

Almost simultaneously, a miniature shower of granite chips stung Patton's right hand; one triangular sliver driving deep into the posterior portion of the metacarpus, another slashing across his right cheek.

Patton swore at the pain and quickly retraced his steps. He crouched behind the granite outcrop, hoping he was out of the bushwhacker's sight. When a second shot failed to come, he felt safe enough to examine his wounds. The cut on his face was minor; he'd knicked himself more severely while shaving. But his hand was much worse; it was bleeding profusely. The tiny rock dagger protruding from the injury needed to be extracted and a bandage applied immediately. He tried to pull the sliver out with his left hand, but it was stuck fast in the last metacarpal. That, and the blood making the stone too slick to grasp and hold on to, made it nearly impossible to remove. Another idea struck him. He bent and twisted his arm until he could get the rock blade to his mouth, where he took it firmly between his teeth, his lips awash with blood that also trickled down his chin. Then he yanked his hand away as hard as he could, and the rock came out cleanly. He spat it away, then reached inside his coat for a handkerchief, removed it, wrapped it around his wounded hand, then tied it as tightly as he could.

Although the pain was excruciating, Patton reached inside his coat and pulled out his gun. Gripping it in his right hand hurt even more, but he had no other choice. To use his left hand would expose him too greatly to the unseen rifleman. Then again, how much good was the revolver to him? The Smith & Wesson had a short range, was meant for close shooting. Out here in the open with his possible target more than likely at least fifty yards away, it could do little else than make the bushwhacker think twice about showing himself.

Patton edged back toward the spot he had just vacated, scanning the upper reaches of the mountain as he did. Nothing in sight. Another short step around the outcropping. Still nothing to see. A little further.

Bang! Instantly followed by *zing!* as the bullet zipped past Patton's head.

The shot didn't frighten Patton. Instead, it steadied his nerves as he held his ground. The flash from the rifle caught his eye. He raised his gun, aimed high, and squeezed off a round. The bullet kicked up dust well below the rifleman's position atop the ridge. Without hesitation, Patton pointed his weapon higher and fired again. This slug ricocheted off a rock closer to its target. The gunman dropped out of sight.

Aware of the fact that his attacker could pop up anywhere along the crest and get off another shot or two—maybe even kill him—before he could return the fire, Patton used military discretion and retreated. But before he could decide what to do next, distant gunfire drew his attention. His head snapped in the direction of the tunnel, but he saw nothing.

"You down there!" shouted someone from the ridge where the rifleman had been. "You're trespassing! Get back where you came from and there won't be no more shooting!"

The other shots had ceased, only to be replaced by incoherent shouting. Evidently, someone else had put Siringo in the same predicament as Patton was in.

"How do I know you won't shoot me on my way down?" Patton shouted back.

"If I'd wanted you dead, I could've killed you twice already!" answered the rifleman. "Now go on your way and I'll leave you be!"

"What about my friend?" asked Patton.

There was no immediate reply, but Patton could hear bits of conversation coming from the crest. The rifleman was conferring with a henchman.

"Your pard's okay!" said the gunman. "He's headed back to your driving machine! You go on now and be on your way!"

Cautiously, Patton peeked around the rocks and saw three riflemen lined up along the ridge. Each one held a Winchester in the military position of inspection arms.

"Okay, I'm going!" shouted Patton.

A few minutes later Patton rejoined Siringo at the Hupmobile.

"You all right, Charlie?" asked Patton.

"I'm fine, but I can see you aren't." Siringo stared at the makeshift bandage on Patton's hand.

"Just a scratch," said Patton. "Piece of rock from a ricochet stuck me."

"Can you drive?"

"Sure."

They drove back to Harqua Hala and called it a day.

"Patton, isn't it?" said Simpson as he entered the room. He closed the door but remained standing.

"That's correct, Mr. Simpson. George Patton, civil engineer."

"Civil engineer you say? Since when do college-educated civil engineers carry guns?"

"Ever since I've been in Arizona."

"I see."

Simpson walked over to the hearth, removed a cigar from a crystal humidor on the mantel, bit off the tip, and spat it into the fireplace. Then he removed a wooden match from the tinderbox beside the tobacco container, struck it on the chimney just below the double-barrel shotgun mounted there, lit the Havana, and tossed the fire stick into the ashpit. After a few strong puffs on the weed, he stalked around the huge oaken desk, sat down in the high-back leather chair as if it were a royal throne, then said, "So what do you want, Mr. Patton?"

"I want to know why your men shot at me and Mr. Stewart yesterday over at Granite Pass."

Simpson sat up straight and leaned forward on the desk. "I don't know what you're talking about, sir."

"Oh, really, Mr. Simpson? Are you denying knowledge of the shooting or are you denying that your company holds claims in the vicinity of Granite Pass?"

"What were you and Mr. Stewart doing out at Granite Pass?" demanded Simpson, ignoring Patton's compound question.

Patton succumbed to the ploy and said, "I'm a civil engineer. I went out there to have a look at the area to consider if it might be possible to straighten the road through the canyon. Mr. Stewart was gracious enough to accompany me. We were climbing the hill over the railroad tunnel when your men started shooting at us."

"If you were on the hill near the railroad tunnel, you were trespassing, and my men had every right to shoot at you. Those are their orders. Keep claim jumpers away."

"Claim jumpers? Do I look like a claim jumper?"

Simpson snickered and said, "Well, not to me, but then I've seen you before. Those men hadn't." He flicked the ash from his cigar into a tray and leaned back with a more relaxed attitude. "Look, Mr. Patton. I'm sorry you were shot at by my men. How can I make it up to you?"

"You can let me get up on that mountain and have a look around," said Patton.

"Is that all?"

"That's it."

"Well, I'll tell you what I'll do, Mr. Patton," said Simpson, suddenly full of cordiality. "I'll take you up there myself and show you around."

Patton was caught off guard. "That's very gracious of you, Mr. Simpson. I'll be around to pick you up with my automobile first thing tomorrow morning."

"Oh, I'm sorry," said Simpson. He took a long puff on the tobacco and blew a large cloud of bluish smoke. "I can't go tomorrow. I'll be busy."

"All right. How about the next day?"

"I'm sorry, Mr. Patton, but I won't be free until the end of next week. I have a gold shipment going out the day after tomorrow, and I'll be riding along with it to Phoenix. I have some business to conduct there. But I'll be perfectly happy to ride out to Granite Pass with you as soon as I get back. Will that suffice?"

"I guess it will have to do."

"Will there be anything else, Mr. Patton?"

"No, I think not," said Patton.

"Then if you'll excuse me, I have a mining company to run."

Patton left the office with more questions than he'd had when he entered; the biggest being: what did Simpson have to hide on that mountain?

FOURTEEN

The curiosities surrounding the murder of Walt Phillips were beginning to trouble Siringo. Each new lead concerning the killing of the deputy turned up a tidbit that in itself raised additional questions. Altogether, they created a mystery that appeared to be taking on conspiratorial dimensions, and this worried the former Pinkerton detective.

Still, Siringo and Earp had come to Harqua Hala for one specific purpose—to find the man who had dry-gulched Walt Phillips in the middle of a June night. They had gathered clues and questioned several unsuspecting people and some who knew they were being interrogated, but out of all the information they had garnered to date, only one item really troubled Siringo.

Patton and Siringo had inspected the murder scene in the dark, and Siringo had been able to confirm some of the details related to Earp by Mamie Sattin. However, a daylight visit to the alley was still necessary in order to confirm the singular fact that Siringo thought he had discovered that night.

Early morning seemed to be the perfect time for Siringo to inspect the alley by sunlight. He slipped out of his room at the Gold House as the first glow of day crowned the eastern horizon. A cool breeze stirred the air. Two roosters in Ditch Town welcomed the dawn, and a dog yapped somewhere near the north end of town. Otherwise, Harqua Hala was still at rest as Siringo strolled casually down the back way to Mrs. Gianelli's boardinghouse.

The sky was a pale blue when Siringo reached the fence around Mrs. Gianelli's backyard. He immediately went to the gate and again looked up at Mamie Sattin's window. His first deduction still held true: the killer had to have stood close to the fence or else Mamie would have seen at least a partial silhouette of the murderer. But that wasn't the fact that bothered Siringo.

On his previous visit, Siringo thought he had recognized two strange indentations in the gate post, but he couldn't be certain about their exact shape in the dark. In the growing light, they turned out to be exactly as he had suspected.

Each one was about a quarter of an inch deep in the wood and somewhat U-shaped—the uppermost gouge upside down. They were about three inches apart, and each one had some sort of design within it. The scars were odd enough, but their position on the gate post struck Siringo as being stranger. They were only three feet from the ground.

As Siringo pondered this curious aspect, the back door to the newspaper building opened, and Horace Beal stepped outside. Barefooted and attired in trousers, suspenders, and undershirt, he yawned and stretched, then commenced to perform a few simple exercises. He sucked in a deep breath upon conclusion of his constitutional, then noticed Siringo for the first time.

"Good morning, Mr. Stewart," said Beal. "What brings you out so early in the morning?"

"Just getting a little exercise, Mr. Beal," replied Siringo. "I always rise early and take a walk before breakfast. Gets the blood going for the day ahead, and the peace of dawn allows the inner man a chance to get a little closer to his Maker."

"An excellent philosophy, sir," said Beal. "I, too, maintain a daily regimen of exercise."

"Yes, I see. Quite commendable, Mr. Beal."

"A good newspaperman has to keep on his toes, especially at this particular time when we're in the midst of a presidential campaign and one of the candidates will soon be in our midst."

"Oh, yes, that's right. Mr. Roosevelt is coming here, isn't he?"

"He's already in the state," said Beal. "His train arrives in Douglas this morning and will stop at Bisbee, Brookline, and Benson before spending the night in Tucson. Tomorrow, he goes on to Tempe and Phoenix. The day after he'll be stopping in Wickenburg, then Salome, on his way to California. No doubt you'll be riding over to Salome to see him when arrives."

"I hadn't given it much thought," said Siringo with all honesty.

"Well, you'd better start thinking about it soon, Mr. Stewart, or you'll miss all the fun. Every man, woman, and child within fifty miles will be in Salome to hear Mr. Roosevelt speak. It's the event of the year."

"Yes, I suppose it is," said Siringo. "I suppose I'll be there as well."

"Be sure to let me know, won't you, Mr. Stewart? I'd like to list you in the *Miner* as one of the area's prominent citizens who will be present."

"I'll let you know, Mr. Beal. For now, I think I'll return to the hotel for breakfast. Good morning, sir."

FIFTEEN

Earp went to work early.

Mamie Sattin and Big George Kramer were standing at the front window when Earp entered the Dutchman's. They were both staring intently at something across the street. Earp joined them, curious about what they were watching.

Deputy Jake Poole was standing in the shade of the boardwalk in front of Hargrove's Mercantile, his hat in hand as he spoke with a young woman. Earp had seen them together as he came down the street but had thought little of the scene. Now seeing Mamie and Big George so interested in the young people intrigued him.

"You two seeing something I'm not?" inquired Earp.

"Jake Poole and Charlotte Simpson," said Big George as if that was all Earp needed to know.

"So?"

"So he's been trying to court that girl ever since she came to town," said Mamie.

"And she's been playing him for a sucker," said Kramer. "She's been seeing Hans Friedkin at night."

Earp already knew this, but Big George didn't know that he knew. And there was no reason to let on otherwise.

"Is that so?" asked Earp innocently. "Does Poole know about Miss Simpson and Friedkin?"

"If he does," said Kramer, "he doesn't let on. Young fool is too smitten with her to see it for himself, and no one's got the heart to tell him."

Just then, Friedkin made an appearance on the street, walking straight toward Poole and Charlotte.

"This ought to be interesting," said Mamie.

Poole saw Friedkin approaching, and Charlotte turned to see what had taken the deputy's attention from her. Seeing Friedkin, she instinctively put a hand to her mouth in surprise, her violet eyes blooming with fear. The young miner halted in front of the couple, tipping his hat to the lady the same as he would to any woman he might casually meet during the day.

"Just keep moving along," said Poole.

"I believe this is a free country, Mr. Poole," said Friedkin, "and since I am breaking no laws, you have no right to tell me what to do."

"You're creating a public disturbance," said Poole, "and—"

"Jake Poole," said Charlotte, "there's no need to be rude. Mr. Friedkin was simply—"

"You stay out of this, Miss Charlotte! This is between him and me."

"That's no way to talk to a lady, Mr. Poole."

"I've already told you to move along, Friedkin, or I'll arrest you for causing a public disturbance."

"You talk boldly when you have that badge on," said Friedkin. "How brave are you without it?"

Poole eyed the miner keenly, then said, "So you want to fight, is that it?" He patted the butt of his gun. "Anytime you feel lucky, Friedkin, I'm willing to oblige."

"I do not fight with guns," said Friedkin.

"Then you'd like me to whip your hide with my fists."

Friedkin smiled and said, "We shall see who whips who." He started to remove his hat and vest.

Poole threw the first punch, knocking Friedkin to the ground with a solid right to the jaw before the miner was prepared to defend himself.

"You uppity foreigner!" snarled Poole. "It's time you were put in your proper place." He quickly took off his coat, hat, and gun belt, dropping them carelessly on the boardwalk.

Clear of his hat and vest, Friedkin was on his feet and storming back, throwing himself bodily at the deputy, crashing the two of them into the front door of the mercantile store, shattering the glass. They went down in a heap, both men swinging wildly and hitting little of the other. They rolled one way, then the other, grunting and straining with every breath.

Charlotte moved aside and watched the contest with intense fascination, intrigued and delighted that two men would come to blows over her.

As word of the fight rippled through the community, the street began to fill with people. Quickly, the crowd broke into three factions: out-of-work miners and the children and wives of miners cheering on Friedkin; a few businessmen and their associates rooting for Poole; and neutrals such as Earp, Kramer, and Mamie Sattin displaying little emotion at all.

Horace Beal arrived just as the combatants rolled into the street, separated, jumped to their feet, and squared off. The newspaperman pushed his way through the human circle that had formed around Poole and Friedkin, then edged around its inner row until he came to Earp.

"Who started it?" asked Beal.

"Poole threw the first punch," said Earp, his eyes not leaving the fighters.

"Shouldn't someone try to stop them?" asked Beal nervously.

"What for?" asked Earp.

"One of them might get killed," said Beal.

"Not likely," replied Earp. "No knives or guns, and the way they're going at it, neither one of them is likely to get hurt much."

Earp spoke too soon.

Friedkin landed a left-right combination and sprawled the deputy in the dust. Poole scooped up a handful of dirt and threw it in Friedkin's eyes, then took advantage of the miner's temporary blindness and landed several unanswered blows to Friedkin's head and body, finally knocking him into the crowd, where he had enough time to regain his sight. Friedkin came charging back, butting his head and right shoulder into Poole's midsection, knocking the wind from him. Poole doubled up and went down into a sitting position, holding his belly in both arms. Friedkin took the initiative and slugged Poole squarely in the jaw, flattening the deputy on his back. Now in a full rage, Friedkin jumped on the semiconscious lawman, his knees pinning Poole's arms as he sat on Poole's chest and began strangling the deputy.

The onlookers emitted a collective gasp as everyone suddenly realized that Friedkin meant to kill Poole. But no one moved to stop him immediately.

"Stop it, Hans!" shouted Beal. With catlike quickness, he broke from the circle and pounced on Friedkin. "Stop it, I say! Stop it now, Hans, before you kill him and spoil everything!"

Friedkin refused to release his victim.

Beal wrapped an arm around the miner's throat and pulled him backward. "Stop it, Hans! You're killing him!"

Big George Kramer finally stepped in, and with one punch from his huge ham of a fist, he knocked Friedkin unconscious.

Earp came forward to see about Poole.

"Is he breathing?" asked Kramer.

"No," said Earp. Without hesitating, he grabbed Poole's belt and jerked the man off the ground a foot or so and immediately dropped him. Then he repeated the action.

"What the hell are you doing, Eagan?" demanded Kramer.

Earp gave it a third try; this time getting the desired result as a noticeable *oof!* puffed from Poole's lips, followed by a series of coughs mixed with intermittent gagging.

"He'll live," said Earp.

Mamie and Big George helped Poole to his feet and started him toward the Dutchman's.

Earp glanced over at Friedkin to see Beal and Charlotte Simpson tending to the miner. He couldn't be certain, but he thought he heard Charlotte ask Beal why he had interfered. Then Beal's angry response seemed to confirm it.

Wondering what was behind the verbal exchange, Earp moved away slowly, stopped, then went back into the Dutchman's. He halted just inside the door, turned, and looked back at the street.

Beal and Charlotte were helping Friedkin, and Big George and Mamie were aiding Poole. For some odd reason, the scene didn't look right to Earp. It was as if Friedkin and Poole were being tended by the wrong people.

SIXTEEN

Patton and Siringo missed the excitement in town because they were in Salome making telephone calls.

Feeling that a letter would take too long to reach Masterson in New York, Siringo opted to place a long-distance call to the former Kansas lawman to request his assistance.

"Hello, Bat?"

"Who's this?"

"Charlie Siringo, Bat. Out in Arizona."

"Charlie Siringo? In Arizona?"

"That's right, Bat. How are you doing there in New York?"

"Making a living, Charlie. How's it by you? What are you doing in Arizona?"

"I'm here with Wyatt Earp," said Siringo.

"Wyatt Earp?" queried Masterson. "How is that old cardsharp?"

"He's fine, Bat. We're both fine."

"Well, what are you two doing out there in Arizona? Still chasing Cassidy and Longbaugh?"

"Not this year, Bat. We're here to investigate a murder for Clyde Farnsworth," said Siringo.

"Farnsworth? Don't believe I know him. Who is he?"

"An old friend of Earp's. He's sheriff of Yuma County. Someone put a load of buckshot in the belly of a deputy—Walt Phillips—and Farnsworth asked Earp to find the bushwhacker. Wyatt asked me to help him because Walt Phillips was an old friend of mine. So we're here trying to find his killer."

"Having any luck?" asked Masterson.

"We know Ben Kilpatrick is in town under an alias."

"Ben Kilpatrick? That killer who rode with Cassidy and Longbaugh?"

"That's him. He's a hired gun for a mine owner named Simpson, Ardmore Simpson. Name mean anything to you?"

"Cripple Creek," said Masterson. "Shyster lawyer who was involved in a mine swindle back about twenty, twenty-five years ago. He bought a played-out mine, salted it, then sent off a big shipment of gold to Denver in the middle of winter. Only trouble was it never got there. Everyone figured an avalanche got the wagon, the driver, and all the guards. Simpson collected from the insurance company, then left town. When spring came and the snow melted, the sheriff found the wagon and the locked strong-box but no bodies. He opened the strongbox and found it filled with lead bars instead of gold. Of course, by this time, Simpson had sold the mine and left town. Sheriff put out paper on him, but no one ever heard of him again. Not till now, that is. You say he's there in Arizona?"

"That's right, Bat."

"And you say he's got Ben Kilpatrick working for him?"

"Right again."

"I'd say you got some real trouble, Charlie. Kilpatrick know you're there?"

"Wyatt and I are using phony names. So far, only two people in town know who we are and what we're doing here."

"Can you trust them?" asked Masterson.

"One's an Army officer who's here on a secret military matter, and the other is Mamie Sattin."

"Mamie Sattin? Telluride, right?"

"That's the one," said Siringo.

"You're all right with Mamie."

"I'm not so sure about that, Bat. Mamie's at the top of my list of suspects right now."

"Mamie a killer? I don't believe it!"

"It's a possibility, Bat, but like I said, she's at the top of the list. I've got at least a half dozen more, and I was hoping you might be able to tell me a little about one of them."

"Who's that, Charlie?"

"His name is Hans Friedkin, a for—"

"Say no more, Charlie. I know him. Bolshevik. Real good trou-blemaker, that one. He was mixed up with some anarchists a few years back who were plotting to blow up the Statue of Liberty. Their Bolshevik newspaper called it a lie, said it was 'a false state-ment' on freedom. They stole some explosives from the Naval Weapons Depot over in Brooklyn, and one of them was caught when he tried to blow up a bawdy house up in the Bronx. Seems he thought the place should have offered free visits." Masterson chuckled as he continued. "He went in waving a stick of dynamite around and demanding service, but he didn't know that the precinct captain and a couple of lieutenants were upstairs at the time. They didn't take too kindly to having their evening entertainment interrupted. They hauled him into the precinct house and worked him over until he told them where he got the dynamite. He told them about Friedkin and the rest stealing it from the Navy, and they rounded up the whole bunch except for Friedkin. He got away clean.

"This is the first I've heard of him since then. What's he up to out there? Is he one of your suspects, Charlie?"

"He's on the list," said Siringo. "He's been stirring up the miners out here against Simpson."

Masterson burst out with a raucous laugh, then said, "I wish I was there to see that."

"It's better, Bat. Friedkin is sneaking around with Simpson's daughter."

Masterson laughed all the louder. "That is rich, Charlie. You and Wyatt must be having a real time of it. A shyster lawyer turned embezzler, a hired killer, a bawdy-house madam, and a Bolshevik troublemaker tied up in a murder case. What else have you got?"

"A banker who may be short in his accounts and a newspaper publisher who's playing Cupid for Friedkin and Simpson's daughter. Then there's the new deputy, a young hothead named Poole who thinks he's you."

It was all Masterson could do to control himself. "Charlie, this is too rich."

Siringo failed to see the humor in it. "Bat, there's one more thing."

"What's that, Charlie?"

"I think Friedkin came here because of Simpson's daughter. It seems she was attending a boarding school for girls up your way until she was kicked out over some man. That was last winter just about the time Friedkin showed up here, and from what Mamie tells us, the Simpson girl and Friedkin started up with each other almost as soon as he hit town. I was hoping you could find out from the school some of the particulars for me."

"Sure thing, Charlie. What's the Simpson girl's first name?"

"Charlotte."

"And what's the name of the school and where is it?"

"Madame duMont's School for Girls in New Rochelle," said Siringo. "I understand that's fairly close to New York City."

"Just up the road a piece," said Masterson. "I'll take a train out there right away and pay Madame duMont a little visit for you. After I do, how do I get back to you?"

"You can call me here in Salome. George and I will hang around here until just before sundown. That's about ten hours from now. Is that long enough for you to get out to the school and back?"

"That's plenty of time. Where do I call you in Salome?"

It was Siringo's turn to laugh. "There's only one telephone here, Bat. At the train depot. Ask for Clayton Stewart. That's the name I'm going by here. I'll be waiting for your call."

They broke the connection, and Siringo placed his next call to the county sheriff's office in Yuma.

"Good to hear from you, Charlie," said Farnsworth. "I got that information you wanted on the Triple H Land Company. I think you'll be as surprised as I was when you hear who owns it. Are you ready for this?"

"Let me have it, Clyde."

"Malcolm Caswell, Horace Beal, George Kramer, and—here's the chaser—Walt Phillips."

Siringo sucked in a deep breath and let it out slowly, saying, "Malcolm Caswell, Horace Beal, George Kramer, and . . . Walt Phillips? Are you sure?"

"Hit me the same way, Charlie."

"I can believe Caswell being an owner," said Siringo. "Him being a banker, that's understandable. And George Kramer, I can believe he could be an owner. But as a partner with Caswell? And Beal? I don't believe I've ever heard of a newspaperman who had more than two bits on him at any one time in his whole life. And him in partnership with Caswell and Kramer? I can believe Beal and Kramer together, but not Beal and Caswell. And all three of them together? It's almost preposterous!"

"And don't forget about Walt being a part of it," said Farnsworth.

"That's really confusing me, Clyde. I can't figure how Walt would be mixed up with Caswell and Beal. Now, I can understand how he and Kramer might become partners in a deal. But the two of them with Caswell and Beal? That's a hard one. How do you figure it, Clyde?"

"Well, I'm one up on you, Charlie," said Farnsworth. "It seems this partnership was formed back in '02."

"Then that may explain it," said Siringo. "They might have been different men ten years ago. This town was more prosperous back then, wasn't it?"

"Quite a bit more. Harqua Hala even had an opera house back then. Well, it wasn't much of an opera house. It was an outdoor stage where traveling shows put on their acts. There was even talk that Eddie Foy was coming once. Never did, though."

"Then I can understand how Caswell, Beal, and Kramer might start up a land company, but I still can't figure where Walt would get the kind of money necessary to buy in with those three. Now I know this might be a little hard to take, but I have to ask. Walt wasn't skimming the tax collections, was he?"

"For all the years I knew Walt," said Farnsworth, "I never knew him to take advantage of his position with the law. But I can understand why you had to ask that. Fact is, I thought you might ask that, so I did some figuring, Charlie. Walt was deputy in Harqua Hala for eighteen years. Over that time, he collected about $3,000 in commissions on taxes, and his wages were $720 a year. That comes to around $16,000. His commission for tax collecting was only three mils on the dollar. Best year he ever had was back in '96, when he took in almost $400 for himself. That's a little over half a year's wages. Since the county provided him with living quarters, he only had to buy his own food and clothes. The county even gave him an allowance for his horse and other trappings necessary for the job."

"What you're saying is, Walt could have saved $5,000 over that time, is that it?"

"Right."

"But that doesn't explain how he came to be partners with Caswell, Beal, and Kramer or how he came to own those mining claims over by Granite Pass."

"I see what you mean."

"Speaking of the money," said Siringo, "have you come up with a way to ask Caswell for it yet?"

"I asked the county attorney to draw up a will for Walt that names me as Walt's executor. He should have it ready for me today, and I'll bring it with me when I come up there tomorrow to set up things for Roosevelt's visit. Instead of driving up in this heat, I'm taking the long way around by riding the night train to Phoenix, where I'll switch trains for Salome. I'll be arriving around midday. I'll get a horse from Sheffler and ride over to Harqua Hala in the afternoon. I'll see Caswell right away and find out about the money. Then I'll have to come back to Salome right away to set things up for Roosevelt's visit. How do I let you know what happens with Caswell?"

"I'll be staying here in Salome tomorrow night," said Siringo. "Just look me up here."

"Okay, I'll see you in Salome tomorrow night."

Siringo said good-bye and ended the call.

It was Patton's turn to use the telephone. He hadn't reported to the provost marshal since arriving in Harqua Hala, and Siringo advised Patton to communicate with him, if for no other reason than to make contact and let Colonel Hardesty know that he was alive and well and on the job.

"Colonel Hardesty, Lieutenant Patton here, sir."

"Yes, Patton, I was wondering when you'd be reporting in. So tell me. What have you learned so far?"

"Well, sir, I haven't learned too much yet, but I believe I've found Benjamin Keenan. He's going under the name of Benteen in Harqua Hala. He works for a mining company as a personal guard for the owner."

There was silence on both ends of the line for a moment. Patton was finished with his report, but the colonel expected to hear more.

Finally, Hardesty said, "Is that all, Lieutenant?"

"Yes, sir," stammered Patton, "I'm afraid so."

"But what about the canister? Have you found the phosgene?"

Patton swallowed hard and said, "I haven't been able to locate it yet, sir."

"But if you've found the man who killed Sergeant Rieger, why haven't you found the canister?"

"Well, sir, I haven't been able to . . . uh . . ."

"Go on, Lieutenant," said Hardesty. "You haven't been able to what?"

"Well, sir, I don't know," stammered Patton. "I wouldn't have found out about Keenan being Benteen if it wasn't for Mr. Siringo and Mr. Earp, sir."

"Who?"

Patton realized that he had made a mistake, but there was no going back now.

"Mr. Siringo and Mr. Earp, sir."

"Siringo and Earp? Who are they?"

"Wyatt Earp, sir?"

"Wyatt Earp? The famous lawman?"

"The same, Colonel."

"I thought he died years ago," said Hardesty. "Why, he must be older than the hills by now."

"He may be up in years, sir, but he's still a hell of a man, sir, if you'll pardon the expression, sir."

"I suppose, if you say so, Patton. What about this other man? Siringo, was it?"

"Charles Siringo, sir. Mr. Siringo is a former Pinkerton agent, sir. He's the man who chased Butch Cassidy and the Sundance Kid out of the country."

"Oh, he's that Siringo," said Hardesty. "What are they doing in Harqua Hala?"

"They're investigating the murder of a deputy sheriff, sir."

"So how do they fit into your investigation? You haven't told them about it, have you?"

There was no way Patton could lie. Hesitantly, he said, "Yes, sir, I have."

"Patton, have you lost your senses? This is a top secret military matter. Your orders were to—"

"Colonel, I know what my orders were," said Patton, slightly irritated, "but I only confided in Mr. Earp and Mr. Siringo because I felt I needed their help. After all, sir, I'm an Army officer, not a policeman or a detective. If not for them, I wouldn't even know about Benteen."

"All right, Patton, take it easy now. There's no reason to be insubordinate. I understand your position, and I know this isn't an easy assignment for you. Just the same, you're supposed to maintain secrecy about this matter. You've failed to do that by telling these two men about the canister. I should recall you immediately, but I'm not so sure that will accomplish anything at this juncture. No, I think not. But I want some action on the canister, Patton, and

I want it soon. That gas is dangerous, and in the wrong hands, a lot of people could get hurt. If this man Keenan . . . or Benteen . . . or whatever his name is—if he was willing to kill the man who stole the canister for him, there's no telling who he might kill next. What about this man he works for? Who is he?"

"His name is Simpson, sir," said Patton. "Ardmore Simpson. He owns the Harqua Hala Mining Company. I can't say for certain whether he's involved or not, but Mr. Siringo and I had some trouble the other day with some of Simpson's guards near the railroad tunnel at Granite Pass. Simpson has some mining claims in the area, and when Mr. Siringo and I went near them, some of Simpson's men started shooting at us. Mr. Siringo believes Simpson has something to hide out there, but we don't know what. I talked to Simpson about it, and he promised to take me out there personally and show me around as soon as he returns from a business trip to Phoenix. By that time, I suppose he'll have hidden anything he might have to hide out there."

"You're probably right about that, Patton. In the meantime, I'll see what I can dig up about this Simpson. You said his name was Ardmore Simpson?"

"Yes, sir."

"Okay, I'll find out what I can, and I want you to call me back in two days. In the meantime, find that canister."

"Yes, sir."

"Oh, I almost forgot," said Hardesty. "A friend of yours from the Academy, a Captain William Mitchell, arrived here yesterday."

Patton was suddenly excited. "Billy Mitchell? What's he doing at Fort Huachuca?"

"He landed on the parade ground in an aeroplane. Created quite a stir. No one around here has ever seen an aeroplane before. Mitchell's on leave, and he's flying around the country from camp to camp trying to drum up support for his plan to get the Army to start an air corps. He came in here looking for you, and I told him you were away on a special assignment. He'll be leaving tomorrow for Fort Ord, California."

"That's too bad," said Patton. "I haven't seen Billy in five years."

"You find that canister, Patton, and I'll see to it that you get an extra leave, and you can go visit Mitchell at Leavenworth."

"Leavenworth, sir?"

"That's where he's headed with the attitude he's got," said Hardesty. "I've never met a junior officer who talked to his superiors the way your friend Mitchell talked to me. You would have thought I was the junior officer and he was a general."

"That's Billy, all right," said Patton with a light chuckle. "He comes from a wealthy family in Wisconsin. I guess he's—"

"Never mind all that, Lieutenant. You just tend to your own job and find that canister."

"Yes, sir."

Their telephoning at an end, Patton and Siringo retired to Sheffler's to await Bat Masterson's return call.

SEVENTEEN

Two and two are supposed to equal four, but Siringo's sum total of evidence was reaching odd proportions.

"The more I learn about these people," said Siringo to Patton as they stood beside the Hupmobile, preparing to return to Harqua Hala that evening, "the less I think I know about who shot and killed Walt Phillips. And as for your case, I don't know what to tell you. I would have sworn Kilpatrick—or Benteen, as he calls himself now—I would have sworn he was your man. Now I'm not so sure. From his past record as an anarchist, I would have to say Friedkin is your man, not Benteen.

"Then there's this business of the Triple H Land Company," he said, continuing. "How do you figure that one? Caswell, Beal, Kramer, and Walt Phillips as partners! Who would have guessed that one? Not me, I'll tell you. Of course, they set up that company a long time ago. Who knows what was going through their minds then? Right now, I don't feel like I'm any closer to Walt's killer than I was the day Wyatt and I arrived in Harqua Hala. All I do know is, I'm as weary as they come, like I've been on the trail for a month and I'm no closer to catching what I'm chasing than I was when I set out. In a word, George, I'm baffled."

"Maybe Wyatt can shed some light on all this," said Patton hopefully. "Maybe you've got so many facts now that you can't see the one thing that will point you in the right direction."

"You mean I can't see the forest through the trees? Is that it?"

"Something like that."

"Okay, let's forget about Walt's killer for the moment," said Siringo. "Let's talk about this gas of yours. You say it's deadly, right?"

"Very deadly. From what I've been told, that one missing canister is enough to wipe out a whole battalion. Explode it in a town like Harqua Hala and it'll kill half the population."

"That's deadly all right. The thing I've been wondering about is:

what would someone do with a thing like that except use it in a war? Got any ideas on that one, George?"

"At first, we thought it might have been stolen by some Mexican revolutionaries. You know how those people are south of the border. There's always some pretty bandito who fancies himself as the savior of Mexico. Then we found out about Sergeant Rieger being murdered in Phoenix and the man he was seen with. That changed Colonel Hardesty's thinking a little bit. He then started thinking that it was an agent of a foreign government who had purchased Rieger's cooperation, but he quickly discarded that idea when we found out the unknown man was from Harqua Hala."

"Hold it right there, George. Let's think about that one for a second. Suppose Harqua Hala is just a ruse. Suppose the sergeant's killer really is a clever foreign agent who just put down Harqua Hala on the hotel registry in order to throw off whoever might come after him. Did your colonel think of that one?"

"Yes, he did," said Patton. "The hotel clerk said the man in question spoke like any other American. Absolutely no trace of an accent. That's why Colonel Hardesty discarded the idea of a foreign agent."

"All right, I can go along with his thinking there, and that sort of puts Friedkin out of the picture. He's a foreigner, and although he doesn't have much of an accent, I'm sure the clerk would have noticed something in his voice. So let's now suppose that Benteen is the man who killed the sergeant and took the gas canister from him. What would Benteen want with it?"

"Maybe we should back up a bit, Charlie," said Patton. "Colonel Hardesty posed this question when we first learned that the canister was missing and Sergeant Rieger was dead. He said, 'How did anyone outside the Army find out about the gas in the first place?' Then he asked, 'How did anyone outside the Army find out the gas was at Fort Huachuca?' "

"And did he come up with any answers?" asked Siringo.

"He checked into Rieger's background first and came up with only one substantial fact. One of Rieger's friends told the colonel about Rieger's drinking problem, and like most drunks, he talked a lot. The colonel surmised Rieger told someone, possibly the same man who killed him, and that's how the information about the gas got out."

"Makes good sense to me," said Siringo. "Did anyone try to find out if Rieger had any civilian friends?"

"Rieger did most of his drinking off the post, most often going all the way to Bisbee to tie on a jag. A check of the saloons in Bisbee failed to turn up anything substantial. None of the bartenders could recall him being too friendly with any of the local men. One of them did say he remembered how Rieger was the big loser in a poker game with a couple of strangers, but he couldn't recall any names, only that they were older men and one of them was dressed to the nines."

The light came on. Patton and Siringo exchanged looks, each knowing what the other was thinking. It was up to Patton to say it.

"That's the same thing the hotel clerk in Phoenix said about the man Rieger had been seen with there."

"And his name was Benjamin Keenan from Harqua Hala," said Siringo. "George, I think you should call your colonel again and ask him to put that name to that bartender in Bisbee. And if that doesn't shake up his memory, maybe mentioning Benteen or Harqua Hala might help."

"Good idea, Charlie. And I might also ask him to find out if the bartender can remember exactly when it was that this poker game took place."

They went back into the train station. Patton placed the call but couldn't reach Hardesty, so he told a subordinate to pass on the information.

The two investigators then climbed into the Hupmobile and started back to Harqua Hala. They passed the evening stagecoach at the beginning of the foothills as the sun dipped slowly below the westernmost peaks of the Harqua Halas. The incline was gradual into the first three curves, then the road swooped down through an arroyo before shooting up a steep rise that leveled out in a straightaway past Big Painted Rock.

Neither man heard the crack of the rifle over the engine noise, only becoming aware of the fact that someone was shooting at them when the bullet exploded through the windshield, leaving a sunburst of a hole behind in the glass as the sole evidence of its passing. Siringo stiffened instantly but recovered just as rapidly, reaching inside his coat for his weapon, the reaction of years in the saddle in pursuit of lawbreakers. Patton went rigid; his grip tightened on the steering wheel and his right leg stiffened, jamming his foot against the accelerator. The car leaped ahead, a saving grace for the auto's two occupants as a second slug zipped behind their heads.

The road swung into another curve and dipped into a gully, affording Siringo and Patton cover from the bushwhacker. Siringo motioned for Patton to stop the vehicle, and the younger man did so, pulling the Hupmobile off the trail close to the protecting ridge. In a second, both men alit, guns at the ready as they crouched against the side of the hill.

"See anyone up there?" asked Siringo.

"I didn't have time to look around," said Patton.

"Me neither. Got any idea where those shots might have come from?"

Patton thought for a second, then said, "They must have come from somewhere behind us. The high ground was off to each side of us, but from the looks of that bullet hole in the windshield, it couldn't have come from either side of the road or from in front of us. It had to have come from an angle behind us."

"Precisely," said Siringo. "I'd say it came from the direction of that big black boulder up there to the left. Most likely only one man with a rifle."

"So what do we do now?"

"We go after him. No one shoots at Charles Angelo Siringo and gets off scot-free. I want the dirty bugger in my sights. You go back up the road a piece, and I'll circle around this way." He waved his gun hand to their right. "If you can get the drop on him, don't hesitate to pull the trigger. Remember, whoever it is up there, he means to kill us. You falter one second too long, and he'll do just that. You get my meaning, George?"

Patton nodded gravely.

"Okay," said Siringo. "Let's go."

The two men moved off in opposite directions.

Patton edged up the roadway in a stoop, sticking close to the hillside. A dozen steps later he was able to see Big Painted Rock in the distance. He could also hear the clippity-clop of the shod hooves of a horse dissipating in the gloaming. Certain that the villain was fleeing, he straightened up and walked casually up the road.

Siringo had hardly started up the draw to the right when he also heard the bushwhacker riding off. He hurried up the hill in the hope that he might still catch a glimpse of the gunman, but luck wasn't on his side. Reaching the crest, he only saw Patton walking toward him from the road.

"Did you see him?" asked Siringo.

"Neither hide nor hair," said Patton.

"Damn! I wish I knew who it was. It just might clear up this mystery a bit." Siringo put his gun away, then said, "Well, let's have a look around. Maybe he left us a clue to his identity."

They searched the area in the fading light and turned up four items: two rifle shells, a footprint, and a swatch of embroidered white cotton cloth stuck to a tiny barrel cactus.

EIGHTEEN

Siringo was still fuming over being shot at when he and Patton returned to the Gold House. He told the young military officer that he wanted to be alone to calm down and think over everything they had learned that day, so he retired to his room for that purpose.

Patton had ideas of his own. The brush with death had only invigorated him; the hound had the scent of the fox's trail, and he wasn't about to stop to sniff the flowers now.

A hot, humid wind blew in from the southwest, bringing with it an ominous cloud of smothering dust; the odor of rain stained the air. Unseen lightning arced in the sky, and thunder rumbled in the distance, hailing the promise of a quenching desert storm and forcing everyone who was wise to the potential danger of the impending atmospheric ferocity to seek shelter.

Although the threat of inclement weather hung over the town, Patton thought it might be the perfect time for spying. Bat Masterson's disclosure that Hans Friedkin had been involved with anarchists planning to blow up the Statue of Liberty had convinced the lieutenant that the troublemaking miner was somehow mixed up with the stolen canister of phosgene. After a quick change of clothes, he slipped out of the hotel through the back door, circled around the building, and headed up the alley toward the rear of the Harqua Hala *Miner.* It was his thought that he just might find Hans Friedkin, Charlotte Simpson, and Horace Beal in conclave in the back room of the publisher's office. The tinny notes of a piano drifted through the night as he passed behind the Dutchman's, then quickly dissipated as he came to the fence gate of Mrs. Gianelli's boardinghouse. He paused to scan the area, and when he was satisfied that no one was about, he crossed the lane to the newspaper office.

Faint yellow light shone through the pulled shade of the only window in the back wall. Patton sidled up to it and put his ear to the glass to hear muffled voices within. He instantly recognized the blustery words of Horace Beal and the confident didactic dictam of Hans Friedkin, but the third speaker was unknown to him. He could only assume the almost inaudible syllables belonged to Charlotte Simpson. Much to his agitation, the howling wind and the increasing cannonade in the clouds distorted their conversation into partial phrases and sentences; he could only hope to catch the gist of what they were saying.

"The old man worries me," said Beal. "He's no cattle rancher from Texas. He's here for something else besides buying and leasing land for a herd of bovines."

"You are probably correct in that assumption," said Friedkin. "The old man is not what he seems to be. He has the air of a lawman about him. He reminds me of those New York police detectives who were constantly snooping around our headquarters. You never knew who you could trust."

"It's the younger one who worries me," said Charlotte. "He looks like a government man to me. You should have heard how he talked to my father the other day. Only someone in a position of some authority would speak to Daddy that way."

Someone else spoke, but Patton could discern neither the words nor the speaker. He wondered if a fourth person were in the room or if Beal or Friedkin had moved to another spot.

"Yes, he raises my suspicions as well," said Friedkin. "The man has nerves of iron, and that makes him a definite threat if he is in league with Stewart and Patton. You have had the best chance to observe him. What is your opinion of Mr. Eagan?"

Again, Patton couldn't hear the person speaking. It annoyed him; it was like reading every other page of a book.

"Yes, I agree," said Friedkin. "During the evening of our little confrontation with the lord of the mine, I overheard old Mr. Higgins talking to Mr. Eagan. Higgins said Eagan looked like some man named Wyatt Earp."

"Wyatt Earp?" scoffed Beal. "Wyatt Earp wouldn't waste his time in a dying town like this. From everything I've ever read about the man, he follows the action. The last I heard of him he was operating a saloon and gambling hall in Goldfield, Nevada. Mr. Eagan may look like Wyatt Earp to old man Higgins, but you can bet your last dollar that your blackjack dealer is not Wyatt Earp."

"Who is this Wyatt Earp?" asked Friedkin.

"Famous gunfighter from the old days," said Beal. "He'd have to be older than Stewart if he's still alive."

"Eagan certainly doesn't look older than Stewart," said Friedkin. "I doubt that he is this gunfighter, Wyatt Earp."

"Then who is he?" asked Charlotte.

"It makes no difference who he is," said Friedkin. "The important thing we have to remember is that, no matter who he and Stewart and Patton are, we have to make certain they are out of our way by the day after tomorrow."

The muffled voice spoke again, and a clap of thunder helped to drown out the speaker.

"If we must, we must," said Friedkin.

"There will be no more killings," said Beal.

"Why did they have to come here now?" asked Charlotte. "Didn't we have enough to contend with already with all of Daddy's men around?"

The muffled speaker spoke.

"Yes," said Friedkin. "At least he is out of the way, and his successor is hardly the same man."

"I still despise him," said Charlotte.

Friedkin laughed, then said, "Still bitter over broken petals, *liebchen?* You were only a child when that happened. It is in the past. Leave it there."

"Never!" snapped Charlotte. "He deserves to die for what he did to me!"

"Never mind that now!" shouted Beal. "We have more important business to tend to here, and we're running out of time to do it. So let's get to the map and go over the plan once more."

Patton could no longer hear what was being said. Either the group inside the newspaper office had moved into another room or they were huddled so close together that soft voices were all that were necessary. Patton suspected the latter.

I'd sure like to get a look at them, thought Patton.

Since he couldn't hear them any longer, Patton worked his way around the building in hopes of finding another window that didn't have its shade pulled down as far as the one at which he had been listening. No luck; the room's other window was covered just as well.

Splat! A giant raindrop smacked Patton on the nape of his neck, startling him. Then a second, a third, and more yet, all pelting the ground, the walls and roof of the building, and Patton, sounding like popcorn roasting over an open flame. Finally, a downpour spilled over the land as the sky released its watery fury on the parched earth.

It would have been folly for Patton to remain any longer; the roar of the storm was too great for him to hear anything above it. The wiser choice of the moment was to seek shelter, and this he did, sprinting for the rear door of the Dutchman's.

Patton was soaked by the time he entered the saloon. He removed his hat and shook the water from it, then brushed at his arms and pant legs. It availed him little; he was still wet when he stepped up to the rail and ordered a shot of brandy to head off the chill he knew would follow if precaution were not applied. He drank it down in a gulp and called for another, which he would take the time to enjoy. The relief bartender poured the second round and left Patton to savor it.

The Dutchman's was fairly void of customers; a couple of miners and Patton. Earp sat at his table reading an old issue of the Harqua Hala *Miner*. Mamie Sattin and two of her girls stood on the balcony, smoking and talking quietly. The barman busied himself by washing glasses.

Patton wasn't sure whether he should engage Earp in a game of blackjack and tell him about spying on Beal, Friedkin, and Charlotte Simpson or remain at the bar and wait for a better opportunity to converse with him. Then again, he didn't know what he should do about the map he heard Beal mention. He decided it would be best to seek the advice of his friend, so he took his drink and sauntered over to the gaming table.

"Good evening, Mr. Eagan," said Patton. "Are you open for business tonight?"

"Certainly," said Earp, folding up the newspaper and setting it aside. He stood and walked around the table and took up the dealer's position. In a lower voice, he said, "Are you looking for a little diversion, George? Or do you want to talk?"

"Talk. Have you seen Charlie since we got back?"

"No. I thought we'd all get together later tonight in the hotel and discuss the situation."

"If we can get back to the hotel through this rain," said Patton. "It's really pouring out there."

"So I see," said Earp, referring to Patton's damp clothing. He began shuffling the deck of pasteboards. "But don't worry about it. Storms out here in the desert don't last that long in the summer. They blow up here from the Gulf of California, drop a lot of rain for an hour or so and cool things off, then move on. Just be sure you're standing on high ground when they hit. The soil can't take all that water in such a short time, so there's always a lot of flooding. Lost a horse once in a flash flood. Danged-fool critter went down into a gulch to get a drink, and a wall of water washed him away. Found him two days later . . . ten miles downstream . . . buzzards eating away at his carcass. Still had my saddle on him. Saddlebags were gone, though. Had to refit myself completely."

Patton glanced around and said, "They're on to us, Wyatt."

Earp stopped shuffling the cards and just stood there for a few seconds, not moving, stunned by Patton's sudden disclosure.

"Who?" asked Earp finally.

"Beal and Friedkin. They know Charlie isn't who he's been saying who he is, and they know I'm not a civil engineer. They think Charlie is some sort of lawman, and they think I'm a government agent. They aren't sure about you yet. At least they don't think you're Wyatt Earp."

"I'm not—" Earp broke off speaking as he saw the two miners heading toward the table. "Make a bet," he ordered.

Patton dug into a vest pocket and pulled out a few coins. He pushed a quarter into the betting circle.

The two miners sat down at the table, and each bet a nickel. Earp dealt a round, and the game continued for the better part of an hour, through the end of the storm.

With the rain stopped and no sign of the two miners wanting to leave the table, Patton lost his patience and decided to wait until he was back at the hotel to relate to Earp and Siringo what he had overheard that evening. He picked up his money and left the same way he had entered the saloon.

The alley was muddy, making walking hazardous. Patton slipped more than once but did not fall as he walked toward the newspaper. He was about to pass the portal in Mrs. Gianelli's fence when the rear exit to the *Miner* opened. Quickly, he opened the gate, stepped into the yard, closed the gate to a crack, then watched the rear of Beal's office.

As he had on the night Patton and Siringo observed the clandestine meeting of Friedkin and Charlotte Simpson, Beal poked his head out and looked around before the first person—Charlotte—exited. Then Friedkin departed.

Patton worried; Friedkin lived at Mrs. Gianelli's. He was trapped in the yard, an open square that measured eighteen feet on each side. What to do? Friedkin was coming his way. His only option was to move to the far corner and hope that Friedkin wouldn't see him when he made his way to the back door of the house. He did so instantly, standing rigid, not even breathing. Nearly a minute passed, and Patton's lungs forced him to exhale. Much to Patton's surprise, Friedkin failed to come into the yard. Now what? Stand motionless all night? How long should he wait to be sure that Friedkin had gone elsewhere? Another minute passed. Patton heard Beal's door close. He waited another minute.

Finally satisfied that Friedkin had gone to a saloon or had chosen to use Mrs. Gianelli's front door, Patton left his hiding place and returned to the gate. He peered through the crack but saw no one. The light was still on at the newspaper, however. Beal was still about. But only for the moment, as Patton saw the light dim, then go out. The diminutive publisher came out and headed for the rear entrance to the Dutchman's.

This was his chance, and Patton knew he might not have an extra second to waste if he wanted to get a look at the map Beal had mentioned earlier. He swung the gate open and hurried across the alley to the newspaper's back door. He tried it. Locked! The window! It slid upward easily. He crawled through and found himself in luck for a change. The room wasn't totally dark; Beal had left a kerosene lamp glowing ever so low. He turned up the flame slightly and began to search for the map.

The room was Beal's personal living quarters, containing a bed and chest of drawers in one corner, an eating table and two chairs in another, a writing desk and chair in a third, and a sofa and rocker in the last. A framed copy of the first number of the Harqua Hala *Miner* hung on the wall behind the couch, and a picture of Karl Marx looked down on the rolltop. A row of books, held upright in line by elephant-head bookends, were atop the desk, which seemed to be the most logical place for Patton to start looking for the map.

Drawer by drawer, shelf by shelf, through every compartment, Patton searched and turned up nothing significant. He looked under the mattress, under the table, the sofa, the chairs; still nothing. Time was slipping away, and he hadn't found a thing. Exasperated, he plopped down on the edge of the bed to think. Where would he hide something if he were Beal? Slowly, he scanned the room. When his eyes came to the picture of Marx, it came to him.

Patton took down the portrait and put it on the desk face down. He removed the back and found—nothing! Angrily, he replaced it and turned to the framed newspaper. He didn't have to remove its back; the map was there. Quickly, he studied the chart, committed it to memory, then returned it to the wall.

His next thought was to exit and find Earp and Siringo as soon as possible. He turned down the flame in the lamp and started to crawl through the window. His right foot touched the ground, and suddenly, a searing pain shot through his neck and brain.

And the dark night became a total blackout for Patton.

NINETEEN

Earp awakened Siringo when he returned to the hotel after work that night.

"Get dressed," said Earp, "and I'll get George up."

Earp went to Patton's room, knocked, but received no answer. He rapped on the door again but still no reply. Odd, he thought; Patton didn't appear to be nocturnally inclined, not a young Army officer, a graduate of West Point, ramrod straight in posture and morals. Uncertain of what to think of Patton's absence, he returned to Siringo's room.

"Where's George?" asked Siringo.

"He's not in his room," said Earp. "I knocked twice, but there was no answer. I wonder where he could be."

Siringo slipped on his boots. "I haven't seen him since we got back from Salome."

"I saw him at the Dutchman's earlier. He played blackjack with me for about an hour while it was raining."

"I thought I heard some thunder and lightning," said Siringo. "Rained you say?"

"Good desert storm. As soon as it was over, George lit out, but he didn't say where he was going. That was about two hours ago."

"Did he tell you someone tried to bushwhack us on our way back from Salome?" asked Siringo.

That caught Earp off guard. "Someone did what?"

"It happened in the foothills. Someone took a couple of shots at us. Put one right through the glass on George's automobile. We tried to get a look at the dirty bugger, but he rode off before we could come up on him." Siringo went to the bureau, opened the top drawer, and took out the two rifle shells and the swatch of white cloth. "We did find these." He handed them to Earp. "What do you make of them?"

Earp examined the evidence, then said, "Looks to me like he used a Winchester .32 Special, and this . . ." He held up the piece of cloth. "This looks like it came from a fancy cuff or a . . . a woman's underskirt. Where did you find this?"

"It was stuck to a cactus. A little one not more than six inches high."

"Looks too clean to have been out there long," said Earp as he returned the three items to Siringo. "You think it belonged to the bushwhacker?"

"That's what I was thinking," said Siringo, "but now I'm finding it hard to believe this came from a lady's undergarment. It makes no sense that a woman would be out there taking shots at us, and no woman I ever heard of—except maybe Belle Starr or Annie Oakley—could have ridden off like that. Even if it did come from a lady's undergarment, it could have been out there for two or three weeks. When was the last time it rained around here? A month ago? Two months? Three? You know how things keep in the desert. Some folks might have been out there on a picnic or something and one of the women might have caught her skirt on that cactus. You never know."

"That's right," said Earp. "You never know. It could have been out there for weeks."

"So what did George tell you?" asked Siringo as he replaced the evidence in the bureau.

"Not much. Only that Beal and Friedkin are wise to us."

It was Siringo's turn to be taken by surprise. "What's this? Beal and Friedkin wise to us?"

"That's what George said."

"Then maybe that explains why someone tried to bushwhack us on the road this evening. They're wise to us, and that means that maybe we're closer to finding Walt's killer than we think we are. Or just maybe we've stumbled into something else."

"Like what?" asked Earp.

"I talked on the telephone with Bat Masterson today, and let me tell you what Bat had to say."

Siringo related his first conversation with Masterson, then told Earp about his talk with Sheriff Farnsworth.

"Then Bat called me back later in the day," said Siringo. "He found out about Miss Charlotte Simpson and why she was dismissed from Madame duMont's School for Girls. It seems Miss Simpson was involved with a man all right. Specifically, one Hans Friedkin. But it wasn't their romantic affair that caused the dismissal. It was Miss Simpson's involvement in Friedkin's anarchist movement."

"But her father is a capitalist," said Earp.

"How many children turn out to be like their parents?"

Earp didn't quite understand, so he asked, "So what do you think all this means?"

"George told me Simpson is shipping some gold tomorrow and that Simpson is going along to do some business in Phoenix. I think Simpson may be planning to steal his own gold just like he did in Colorado. The question we have to answer is: how is he going to do it?"

"Why do you and I have to answer it, Charlie? Simpson is none of our business. We're here to find Walt's killer and that's all. Simpson stealing his own gold is something I think we should leave to Farnsworth."

"I think the robbery may be why Walt was killed," said Siringo. "I think he might have found out about Simpson's plan, and Simpson had him killed."

"You don't think Simpson did it himself, do you?"

"No, he's not a killer. He hires other men to do his killing for him. The question is which one did it. Just because we don't know anything about the others, I'm inclined to think it has to be Kilpatrick. He's the only logical choice at this point."

"But what about Beal and Friedkin?" asked Earp. "How do they fit into all this?"

"I think they may be planning to steal Simpson's gold out from under his nose. After all, they've got Charlotte Simpson to spy on her father for them. It's just possible that she found out about her father's plan, passed it on to Beal and Friedkin, and then they came up with a plan to steal it from him."

Earp couldn't hold back a chuckle. "Charlie, isn't that a little farfetched?"

"I know it sounds like it came out of the south forty," said Siringo, "but the way this thing is shaping up just about anything is possible."

"Well, isn't it possible then that maybe Walt found out about their plan and they killed him?"

"That's possible," said Siringo, "but I doubt it. Other than the Triple H Land Company partnership, there doesn't appear to be any other ties between Walt and those anarchists. And if Walt was involved with them somehow, that would also implicate Caswell and Kramer."

"Speaking of Caswell and Kramer, just how much do we know about those two?"

"Good question, Wyatt. Come to think of it, about all we do know about them is what we've observed of them since we've been here, and that isn't much."

"Maybe we should talk to Mamie about them," said Earp.

"Precisely," said Siringo. "Do you think she might still be awake at this hour?"

"Even if she isn't, I think we should go see her anyway. If Beal and Friedkin are wise to us and if Simpson is planning a robbery tomorrow, we shouldn't waste any time."

"Precisely."

Like thieves in the night, Earp and Siringo left the hotel and walked down the alley to the outside staircase that led to the rooms above the Dutchman's. Before climbing the stairs, they looked up at Mamie's window and saw that a light still glowed there; she was still awake. They knocked softly, and Mamie let them in without a greeting.

"I'm glad you two came here," said Mamie as soon as she closed the door behind them. "I've been sitting here wondering how I could get into the hotel and up to your room without being seen. I've got big news for you."

"Big news?" queried Earp.

"Simpson was up here this evening," said Mamie.

"I didn't see him come into the saloon," said Earp. "When was he here?"

"He used the outside stairs, the same as you did. And he wasn't alone. He and Benteen came up right after the storm."

"Benteen?" asked Siringo.

"That's right," said Mamie. "The big gun himself. They got very drunk, and they were pretty free with their money. They made a real night of it. They're both passed out down the hall right now."

"That sounds like Kilpatrick all right," said Siringo. "That Hole-in-the-Wall Gang used to do the same thing before every job they ever pulled."

"Kilpatrick?" asked Mamie.

"That's right," said Earp. "Benteen is none other than Ben Kilpatrick."

"Well, I'll be," said Mamie. "Wasn't he the one who was tied down to a working girl named Laura Bullion?"

"The same," said Siringo. "He sort of dropped out of sight for a few years. He's still wanted up in Wyoming, but that will have to wait. We've got problems right here and now."

"I'll say you have," said Mamie. "Simpson and Benteen, uh, Kilpatrick . . . they're leaving for Phoenix tomorrow with a shipment of gold."

"We already know that," said Earp.

"Yeah, but did you know that they're going to San Francisco from there?"

"San Francisco?" asked Siringo. "What's so important about San Francisco?"

"They're taking the Flyer," said Mamie, as if that should explain it all.

Earp and Siringo exchanged looks that said they didn't understand, then they looked back at Mamie.

"The Flyer," she repeated. "Don't you get it? They're taking the Flyer."

"I'm sorry, Mamie," said Siringo. "What's so significant about them taking the Flyer?"

"Every gold mine in the territory sends its gold to Phoenix," said Mamie, as if she were explaining a simple math problem to two schoolboys, "and once a week, the Flyer takes it to the mint in San Francisco."

The light came on in their heads at the same time. Simpson, Kilpatrick, and a train loaded with gold. It made sense.

"So that's it!" said Siringo. "Simpson isn't planning to steal his own gold. He's going to steal everyone's gold. A train like that must carry a couple hundred thousand dollars in bullion on it."

"Try a couple of million," said Mamie.

Earp and Siringo let out low whistles.

"But the Flyer must have twenty or thirty guards on it for that much gold," said Earp. "How could they rob a train that well guarded?"

"I don't know," said Mamie, "but Simpson said they had that all taken care of."

"Did he say how?" asked Siringo.

"No. All he said was they'd be snuffed out all at once."

Earp and Siringo looked at each other and simultaneously said, "The gas!"

"The gas?" queried Mamie.

Siringo ignored her question and said, "But how are they going to use it?"

"We've got to find George," said Earp, "so he can alert the Army. This is bigger than we can handle."

"You're right, Wyatt," said Siringo. "We'll have to find George immediately. But first things first. We've still got a killer on the loose, and if today is any indication, he's about to kill again."

"What are you talking about?" asked Mamie.

"Someone tried to bushwhack Charlie and George on their way back from Salome," said Earp.

"Did you see who it was?" asked Mamie.

"No," said Siringo. "He got away clean."

"Mamie, we were talking about this earlier at the hotel," said Earp, "and we were going over the possible suspects when we realized there's a lot we don't know about a couple of fellows who are involved in this mess. We were hoping you could tell us something about Big George and Malcolm Caswell."

"Sure," said Mamie. "What would you like to know?"

"Mamie," said Siringo, "do you know anything about the Triple H Land Company?"

"Sure. It was big news around here about ten years ago. Big George and Walt started it with the idea of making Harqua Hala into a regular city. They bought up a couple of sections just south of town and sank a couple of wells. They were trying to convince some eastern land speculators that there were underground springs here whose waters were healthful. They wanted these Easterners to ballyhoo the place as the Hot Springs of the West. They were going to build a big hotel and a whole bunch of things. Only thing was, the Easterners weren't buying. After a year or so, they gave up on it."

"What about Caswell and Beal?" asked Siringo.

"Caswell and Beal?"

"Yes, what was their part in the venture?"

"Beats me."

"Didn't you know Beal and Caswell were also partners in the Triple H Land Company?"

"This is news to me," said Mamie. "I thought it was just Big

George and Walt. After they were cashiered out of the Army in '98—"

"Wait a minute," said Earp. "Big George and Walt were in the Army?"

"That's right. When the ruckus started down in Cuba, they joined Teddy Roosevelt's Rough Riders."

"Weren't they too old for that?" queried Siringo.

"That's what I said, but they went anyway. They didn't get into the fighting, though. Roosevelt himself took one look at them and made Big George a cook and Walt a supply sergeant. Big George took that hard because Roosevelt called him a tub of lard that would break a horse's back. But Walt didn't mind his job. Sure, he wanted to fight, too, but when he saw so many younger men in the outfit, he knew he was better off in the rear. But not Big George. Roosevelt had insulted him, and he hated him for it. The whole time Roosevelt was President, Big George did nothing but rant and rave about everything Roosevelt did. No matter what it was, Big George said it was wrong."

"What about Caswell?" asked Siringo. "How much do you know about him?"

"Not much. He was here when I got here in '94, and he's been running that bank ever since. Quite a respectable citizen, I guess. He never comes up here, although he's not married. He does drink a bit, but I've never seen him drunk. About the only vice he's got is gambling. I've seen him drop two, three hundred bucks at a clip sometimes. He wins once in a while but not often. You've played with him, Wyatt. You know what kind of gambler he is."

"Yes, I have," said Earp, "and I can tell you he's not much of blackjack player. The man hits stiffs when I've got one showing, and he splits face cards. The sure signs of a man who knows very little about the odds."

"Mamie, did you know the Triple H Land Company bought up a bunch of land over by Salome?" asked Siringo.

"No, I didn't. What's that got to do with Walt's murder?"

"We don't know yet," said Siringo. "I was kind of hoping you might throw some light on it for us."

"Sorry, I can't help you there."

The three went mute for the moment. Silence permeated the whole building. Even the night outside was dead still. Not a creature stirred anywhere in Harqua Hala except for a pair of diamondbacks slithering between the gravestones.

TWENTY

Sheriff Clyde Harrison Farnsworth drew up the reins on the hot and thirsty horses and halted the hired rig in front of the Harqua Hala jail. As the cloud of dust that had followed him all the way from Salome settled around him, he sagged back, heaved a sigh, and felt like just sitting there until someone took pity on him and brought him a cool drink, a stiff one preferably.

Jake Poole saw the sheriff through the office window. He jumped to his feet and rushed outside to greet his superior, completely forgetting he wasn't wearing his boots.

"Sheriff Farnsworth," said Poole, "what are you doing here?"

Farnsworth turned his lowered head slowly and peered over the round lenses of his spectacles. Fatigue dulled the gray flecks in his brown eyes, and the droopy ends of his thick salt-and-pepper mustache accentuated the frown lines of his mouth and chin. His heavy jowls seemed to become too much for his jaw as his lips parted to speak.

"Is that all you can say to me, Poole? 'What are you doing here?' No 'Hello, Sheriff, it's good to see you'? Or a simple 'How are you, Sheriff?' No, I guess not. I guess it's too much to expect from a deputy who runs around without his boots."

Poole looked down at his feet and nervously flexed his toes. Then, embarrassed, he dashed back inside and pulled on his footwear, but before he could run outside again, Farnsworth's stout frame appeared in the doorway.

"Uh, Sheriff," stuttered Poole, "it's . . . it's good to see you again. What . . . uh . . . brings you up this way?"

Farnsworth ignored the question and eased his tired, overweight body into the unpadded oaken office armchair behind the desk. He pulled open the top right drawer, rummaged around, then closed it. He repeated the actions with all the compartments.

"Where do you keep it?" asked Farnsworth.

"Keep what, Sheriff?"

"The bottle, lunkhead! Where do you keep it?"

Poole hesitated, then disappeared into the back room, reappearing a moment later, brandishing a quart of Old Crow. He rushed over to Farnsworth and presented him with the whiskey.

Farnsworth looked at the label, then up at Poole. "This your regular brand, Poole?"

"Oh no, sir, Sheriff. This was left over from Walt's personal stock. I just kept it around for when anyone important should come in."

"Meaning me?"

"Especially you, Sheriff. Walt always told me how you liked your whiskey."

"He did, did he?"

"Yes, sir, he did."

"Well, I don't doubt it. Walt always knew how to take care of a visitor. Join me?"

"Sure thing, Sheriff."

Poole vanished to the rear again, coming back a moment later with two tin cups. He put both down on the desk, broke the tax seal on the bottle, and poured the drinks.

"To Walt," said Farnsworth, lifting his cup in salute. "May we find his killer so he can rest in eternal peace." He drank, downing the liquor in a single swallow.

The deputy hesitated for a noticeable second, then followed his superior's example.

Farnsworth held out his cup for another shot, and Poole obliged him, then himself.

"That one was for Walt," said Farnsworth. "This one's for me and my aching bones." He gulped the drink, then put the cup on the desk. "Now let's get down to business, Poole. I haven't got a lot of time, and I want to get back to Salome before dark."

Poole corked the bottle and returned it and the cups to the back room. In a moment, he was standing in front of his own desk like a schoolboy waiting for the teacher to discipline him.

"Sit down, Poole," said Farnsworth without looking up from a paper he held in his hand in front of him. "You make me nervous standing there like that."

Poole sat in the only other chair in the room.

Farnsworth put the paper into his vest pocket and turned his attention to his deputy. "Jake, what are you doing about finding Walt's killer?"

"Well, I've been keeping my eyes and ears open for clues, Sheriff," said Poole, "but I ain't turned up nothing yet."

"Is that right? Eyes and ears open and you still 'ain't turned up nothing yet.' In all this time since Walt was killed, you haven't turned up a single clue." Farnsworth shook his head with incredulity. "Boy, you amaze me. How can you be so blind? Or so stupid? You've been here all along, every day, and you know everyone in town, and you still can't figure out who might have killed Walt. I mean, you don't even have a hunch about which ten people in town might have done it."

"That ain't so, Sheriff," said Poole in his own defense. "I got a good hunch about who might have killed Walt."

"Is that right? And who does your hunch say it was?"

"Hans Friedkin."

"And what makes you think he did it?"

"He's a Bolshevik, ain't he?"

"A what?"

"A Bolshevik. That's what Mr. Simpson calls him. Mr. Simpson says he a godless Bolshevik."

"Is that right? And you think Mr. Simpson's word is gospel, is that it?"

Poole hesitated, then said, "Well, no, sir. It's just that Friedkin is a troublemaker, and Walt didn't like him from the minute he hit town last winter."

"Did Walt ever tell you why he didn't like Friedkin?"

"Well, not exactly."

"Is that right?" asked Farnsworth. "So what exactly did he say was the reason why he didn't like Friedkin?"

"Well, Walt got drunk one night, and he told me then that he hated the bastard."

"That's what he called Friedkin? A bastard?"

"Well, not exactly."

"Hell, boy, exactly what did he call him?"

"Walt said, 'I hate him, that little bastard of mine.' That's what he said."

"His little bastard?"

"Well, Walt was drunk at the time," said Poole.

"I don't care nothing about that," snapped Farnsworth. "Are you sure that's what he said?"

"Those were his exact words, Sheriff."

Farnsworth sat still for a moment, digesting the deputy's words. He stroked his chin thoughtfully.

"Jake, I want to talk to Friedkin. Go find him and bring him here. I'm going over to the bank to talk to Mr. Caswell for a bit, but I want Friedkin here by the time I get back. You hear me, Poole?"

"Yes, sir, Sheriff. I'll go arrest him right now."

"I didn't say nothing about arresting anyone," snapped the sheriff. "Just you tell him I want to talk to him. You got that?"

"Yes, sir. You just want to talk to him."

"That's right. Now get going."

Poole grabbed his hat and left.

Farnsworth pushed himself from the chair, forced his spine to straighten, then followed his deputy through the door. A few minutes later he was sitting in Malcolm Caswell's office, facing the banker with a keen eye.

"Mr. Caswell, I think you'll find this is all in order," said Farnsworth as he presented the banker with the paper he had perused a few minutes earlier in the jailhouse.

Caswell took the document and read the court order that acknowledged the sheriff as executor of Walt Phillips' estate. With each passing word, Caswell's color grew more and more ashen. He was unaware that he was visibly shaken as he absently allowed the single legal-size page to leave his hand and float down to the desktop.

"Well, Sheriff, being an executor is a big job, especially in this case," said Caswell nervously.

"Why do you say that, Mr. Caswell?" asked Farnsworth.

"Well, everyone knows Walt had no relatives. Without legitimate relatives to claim the estate, discharging its assets becomes quite a problem."

"Mr. Caswell, I have reason to believe Walt did have a relative or two, and as soon as I place all the proper advertisements requesting those folks to contact my office, I'm sure someone will come forward to claim the estate. In the meantime, I'm going to close Walt's account here and take the money back to Yuma, where it will be close at hand." Farnsworth dug into his vest pocket again and pulled out the deposit slip he had found when he searched Walt's possessions right after the late deputy's demise. "From the looks of this, Walt had almost five thousand dollars in your bank." He handed the receipt to Caswell.

The banker was near to being apoplectic. He stiffly accepted the paper and stared hard at the figures scrawled on the bottom line.

"This . . . this must be a . . . mistake," muttered Caswell.

"What's that?" asked Farnsworth.

"Uh, mistake," stammered Caswell. "Yes, that's right," he said, regaining his composure somewhat. "This must be a mistake. I don't recall Walt ever having that much money in this bank."

"That is one of your deposit slips, isn't it?"

"Well, yes, it is, but the figures must be in error. As I just said—"

"I heard what you said, Mr. Caswell. If this is wrong, then exactly how much money did Walt have here?"

Caswell cleared his throat and said, "Well, I can't say offhand. I'd have to check the books."

"I've got a better idea," said Farnsworth. "Why don't I have the county treasurer come up here and help you check your books? That way we can get a better picture of how things are with Walt's account."

Caswell lost what little remaining color he had, but his reactions were perfectly normal as he leaned forward instantly and said, "No-no, we don't need that. We can accommodate you quite nicely, Sheriff, without bringing the county treasurer into this."

"Is that right?" quizzed Farnsworth. "You can get this all straight without the help of the county treasurer?"

"Yes, sir."

"Well, I think it just might be better to have the county treasurer come up here just the same. An extra numbers man around won't hurt nothing. Maybe he can help you straighten out a few other accounts, too."

Caswell wanted to groan but knew he shouldn't. Instead, he said with funereal resignation, "Yes, I suppose that would be a good thing to do."

"There's a few other matters concerning Walt I'd also like you to help clear up for me," said Farnsworth.

"Certainly, Sheriff. Anything to help the law."

"I understand Walt was in partnership with you and a few other gentlemen in the Triple H Land Company. How much of the company did Walt own?"

Caswell flinched and blanched even more before answering hesitantly. "Well, it was . . . it was— Well, Walt was an equal partner," he said, "with Horace Beal, George Kramer, and myself.

We formed the company ten years ago to start a health resort just south of town, but it never amounted to anything. So we took our losses and more or less called it quits."

"When did you buy up those tracts over by Salome?"

The question bludgeoned Caswell's senses, reeling his mind into confusion, sweat effusing from every pore of his skin. He fumbled in his coat pocket for a handkerchief, finally got a grasp on it, and wiped his face with feminine dabs.

"Very hot today, isn't it, Sheriff?"

"It's August," said Farnsworth. "What did you expect? A blizzard?"

Caswell let out a nervous chuckle. "No, of course not."

"What about those tracts around Salome?" Farnsworth kept up the pressure. He had Caswell at the end of a tether, and there was no way he would let the banker off now. A jerk here, a little slack there; play him till he was worn out and ready to capitulate.

"Well, we . . . uh . . . we bought those tracts from the railroad a year or so back. Walt had the idea that we could graze cattle on them."

"Makes sense," said Farnsworth, easing off for the moment. "Lots of grass in that valley in the wintertime. Get a few more wells over there, and you could even irrigate the land in the summer and grow a little hay. Smart thinking, I'd say."

"That's what we all thought," said Caswell by way of a sigh of relief.

"Okay, that covers that. Now what about those mining claims Walt had over in the Harcuvars? What do you know about those?"

"M-mi-mining claims?"

"That's right. Mining claims. Walt had a bunch of them in the Harcuvars. Any mines on them?"

"I wouldn't know about that," said Caswell.

Farnsworth decided it was time to pull him in and lay a brand on his hide where it would burn the most. "Then what do you know about the claims? Didn't Walt deposit some gold dust in your bank on occasion?"

"Yes, I suppose he did, but I don't know where it came from. I just thought he was getting it from gambling. You know, from miners who bet their pokes in a card game."

"Walt hardly ever turned a card for money," said Farnsworth. "But you say he won it gambling?"

"No, I said I just thought that's where he was getting it. I suppose he could have been doing a little mining on his own. Who knows? Walt kept to himself a lot."

"Then why did he go into partnership with you and the others if he kept to himself a lot?"

"Well, he wasn't always like that," said Caswell.

The time had come to trump the ace, and Farnsworth threw down his power card with finality.

"Caswell, I think you're a liar, and I think you've been lying to me the whole time I've been here. So I'll tell you what I'm going to do to get to the truth. I'm closing your bank and taking your books back to Yuma with me for the county treasurer to examine."

"You can't do that!"

Farnsworth leaned forward and snarled, "Don't tell me what I can or can't do, Caswell. I'm the sheriff. I can do anything the law lets me do, and right now I'm closing you down and putting you under arrest."

"Arrest? What for?"

"Embezzlement, for starters. I think you've been stealing from your own bank, and—" Farnsworth was distracted from finishing the sentence by the look on Caswell's face. "Hey, you all right, Caswell?"

The banker didn't answer. His hands struggled to his chest for a second, then they collapsed at his side. Caswell's head lolled to one side, and a morbid sigh wheezed from his open mouth.

Farnsworth sat motionless, at first not knowing what to make of Caswell's condition. Then, after figuring out what had happened, he was mortified that he had frightened the man to death.

TWENTY-ONE

Salome was decked out like the Fourth of July for Roosevelt's impending visit the next day. Brand-spanking-new American flags with forty-eight stars, the last one for Arizona, the newest state of the Union, decorated every possible space available, and where flags wouldn't hang, red, white, and blue bunting dressed up the town with true patriotic fervor.

Although it was the evening before the candidate's arrival, the small railroad stop was already teeming with people wanting to catch a glimpse of the former President and listen to him give a campaign speech from the rear platform of his private campaign coach. Cowboys from the ranches to the north, miners from the surrounding hills and mountains, businessmen from as far away as Yuma and Gila Bend, men of all walks of life, some even bringing their families to see the great man with the winning grin and the pince-nez eyeglasses; they would all be there to greet the famous founder of the Rough Riders, Teddy Roosevelt, the American hero of whom Mark Hanna said upon President McKinley's death, "And now that damn cowboy is President." Every spare room in town was already booked for the night, and when indoor accommodations were no longer available, enterprisers rented tents to those who could afford them and didn't want to travel all the way to Harqua Hala, the only place with a hotel within a two-hour ride of Salome.

Farnsworth returned to this carnival atmosphere an hour before sundown. He went straight to Sheffler's Saloon and sought out Siringo, who had left Harqua Hala while the sheriff was at the bank. Although Siringo had never met him, Farnsworth was sure he would know the former Pinkerton on sight, having seen Siringo at a court trial in Prescott many years before. He walked up to the detective, who was standing at the bar, and introduced himself.

"Mr. Stewart, I'm Sheriff Clyde Farnsworth," he said with a hand extended in greeting.

"How do you do, Sheriff Farnsworth?" said Siringo, accepting the handshake.

"You come here for the doings?" inquired the sheriff.

"Wouldn't miss it for the world," said Siringo. He glanced around the room. "Looks like lots of other folks feel the same way."

"It's a bit crowded here, ain't it? Care to go someplace less busy?"

"Lead the way, Sheriff."

Farnsworth called the proprietor over, ordered two iced beers, and inquired whether the back room was available. Sheffler said it was, then drew the brews, giving them frosty heads. The mugs were already sweating when he set them down in front of the sheriff. Each man picked up one, then Farnsworth led Siringo to the private chamber in the rear of the saloon.

The room was sparsely furnished with four wooden chairs around a square table. Nothing adorned the walls, not even windows. A second door permitted exit to the outdoors.

Siringo and Farnsworth sat down across the table from each other, raised their glasses in a toast, drank a long swallow, then leaned back to talk.

"You can scratch Malcolm Caswell off your list of suspects, Charlie," said Farnsworth. "He's dead."

"Dead?"

"Heart, I think. Could've been apoplexy. Who knows? All I know is, we were talking in his office when all of a sudden he keels over deader than a doornail. I wonder if it was something I said."

"What did you say to him, Clyde?"

"I confronted him with what you told me, and the more I talked about it, the grayer he got. Then all at once—well, not all at once—but it was quick. Anyway, I was telling him I thought he was a liar and I was arresting him for embezzling from his own bank when he up and croaks on me right then and there. It is not a pleasant sight, Charlie, to watch a man go that way. Not pretty at all."

"Did he say anything before he died that might help us find Walt's killer?" asked Siringo.

"He confirmed the partnership of the Triple H Land Company, but that's about it. When I asked him about Walt's money, he claimed there had to be some sort of mistake in the deposit slip, and when I asked him about Walt's mining claims, he denied knowing anything about them. I think he was lying."

"That's not much help, Clyde."

"Well, maybe that's not, but let me tell you something else I found out when I was in Harqua Hala." Farnsworth leaned forward in a conspiratorial manner. "Walt had a bastard son."

"Yes, we know," said Siringo.

"You know? How do you know that?"

"Mamie Sattin told us about an indiscreet liaison she had with Walt when she was quite young, and a child was the result. She left it with an immigrant couple and never saw it again."

"Well, I found him," said Farnsworth.

"You found him? In Harqua Hala?"

"That's right. Walt's bastard son is none other than Hans Friedkin."

"Hans Friedkin? But— No, I see now. Yes, it makes sense. But how did you find out?"

"Jake Poole told me."

Siringo was incredulous. "That buffoon? But how—"

"He didn't even realize what he was saying," said the sheriff. "What he did was repeat something Walt said when he was drunk once. He said Walt told him, 'I hate him, that little bastard of mine.' That's exactly what Poole said. I told him to find Friedkin and bring him to me so I could question him about it, but the simpleton couldn't find him. He asked around, and someone told him that Friedkin had already left town for the festivities over here."

"Well, if he's here, I haven't seen him yet," said Siringo. "You know, Clyde, a story like that coming from someone like Poole will have to be confirmed. We'll have to talk to Mamie again, and of course, we'll have to question Friedkin. If they confirm Poole's story, then it looks to me like we've got us a first-class suspect.

"But that will have to wait for the moment, Clyde. You've got a bigger problem on your hands."

"Is that right? You don't know the half of it. Putting on all these extra deputies to guard Roosevelt is a real pain in—"

"That's not your problem, Clyde," said Siringo. "Do you know Ardmore Simpson?"

"The mine owner in Harqua Hala."

"That's him. Did you know he once owned a mine up in Colorado and he arranged to have one of his own gold shipments hijacked on its way to Denver?"

"Is that right?"

"And now we have reason to believe he's planning to do it again," said Siringo.

Farnsworth flinched with surprise. "Is that right?"

Siringo reviewed all the facts as he knew them, then added his own speculations. Farnsworth listened intently, coming to the same conclusions Earp and Siringo already had. There was no doubt about what Simpson was planning, but there were still two questions to be answered. How was he going to steal the gold? And where was he going to steal it?

"I think I know where he's going to steal it," said Siringo.

"Is that right?"

"Simpson has some kind of mining operation going on at Granite Pass. He's got twenty or so men over there."

"Then I better get my deputies over there and round them up now," said Farnsworth. "Stop it now before someone gets hurt."

"What would you arrest them for, Clyde? So far, they haven't done anything wrong that I know of. You ride out there now, tonight, and you just might upset everything. Simpson's the one you want. Scare off his boys, and you just might lose him. There's still time for us to figure out how he's going to steal the gold, and once we do you can be waiting for him."

"You just might have something there, Charlie. Yeah, sure. Find out how he's going to do it and set a trap for him. Yeah, that's what we'll do."

Siringo started to say something, but a sudden, loud roar of a gasoline motor stayed his tongue.

"What the devil was that?" asked Farnsworth.

"Sounded like some sort of automobile," said Siringo.

Then they heard a lot of shouting from the barroom, followed by a stampede of booted feet.

"Whatever it was," said Siringo, "it's sure got everyone stirred up. Maybe we better go see what it's all about."

Both men returned to the bar to see all the customers exiting through the front door. Sheffler and his bartenders remained at their stations, although it was obvious that they were just as eager to leave the saloon as the patrons were.

"What's going on, Sheffler?" asked Farnsworth.

"Someone said it was a flying machine," said the saloonkeeper. "There it is!" someone outside shouted.

Farnsworth and Siringo joined the crowd in the street. Everyone was moving east. Gradually, the sheriff and the detective worked their way through the throng to the forefront.

"Well, I'll be," said Farnsworth.

There in the road, taxiing their way, was a Martin "T" biplane, its single propeller raising an enormous cloud of dust behind it. As it approached, they could see the pilot dressed in a duster, goggles, and a leather cap with earflaps and chin strap. He pulled the plane off the road across from the railroad station and shut down the engine. As he unbelted himself from the open cockpit and climbed down from the aeroplane, the crowd of curiosity seekers surrounded the craft. Farnsworth and Siringo stepped up to him as he removed his protective clothing, revealing an Army cavalry uniform bearing the twin bars of a captain. Upon seeing the sheriff's badge, he removed his headgear and replaced it with a military flat hat, also adorned with the badge of rank.

"Captain William Mitchell at your service, sir," said the pilot as he saluted the lawman.

TWENTY-TWO

Harqua Hala was enjoying the same excitement as Salome; Malcolm Caswell's sudden death failing to dampen anyone's spirits, actually adding to the anticipation of the upcoming event as locals spoke animatedly of the deceased.

The Gold House was filled to capacity and then some. Every saloon was doing a booming business, the Dutchman's being no exception. It was the first really busy night for Earp since his arrival in the mining town, and his players were not the nickel-and-dime miners but out-of-town visitors staying over for the sole reason of seeing and hearing Roosevelt in Salome the next day.

Before going to work, Earp inquired of the hotel clerk about Patton. No, he hadn't seen the young engineer all day; a check of his room proved he hadn't spent the night there either. The lieutenant's disappearance plagued Earp's mind all through the evening.

Also disturbing his concentration was the possible train robbery Ardmore Simpson had to be contemplating. There was no real hard evidence that indicated the mine owner was really planning the theft, only circumstantial proof and history. It was well known that the mine was paying out, and there was the secret mining operation going on at Granite Pass. Was Simpson getting gold from one and passing it off as ore from the other? No, that couldn't be. The only mill in the area was in Harqua Hala, and if Simpson was bringing ore from the Granite Pass mine to it, someone would certainly notice. Then what was he doing with the ore from the secret mine? Or was there any ore there at all? Maybe that was it. Maybe the mine was a ruse. But for what? The operation was near the railroad. So maybe that was it. The diggings were just an excuse to keep a gang of outlaws near the place where he planned to hold up the train. That had to be it.

Once he had resolved that part of the puzzle in his mind, Earp set his thoughts on how Simpson planned to rob the Flyer.

Simpson, Kilpatrick, and four guards had left Harqua Hala early that day. The mine owner and his number one gun drove the ore wagon carrying the strongbox, while the riflemen rode horses, two in front and two in back of the wagon. Without fanfare, they departed the town on Salome Road. Siringo followed them at a distance until he reached Big Painted Rock, where he watched them through binoculars as they covered the last few miles to Salome. He made sure they loaded their cargo onto the eastbound train, then saw the train pull out and the wagon and four riders head off in the opposite direction. Satisfied that Simpson was doing exactly what he said he would, Siringo returned to Harqua Hala to report to Earp.

But the question of how Simpson would rob the Flyer on his return trip continued to nag at Earp. Would he wreck the train? No. Simpson would be on it, so that was out; he wouldn't risk injuring himself. That was it. Simpson would be on the train; it would take very little for him to reach the cab of the locomotive and force the engineer to stop the train at any given spot along the road. Once the train was halted, Simpson's men would swarm all over it and take the gold. No, that couldn't be. The Flyer would be heavily guarded. A shoot-out was too risky, and that wasn't Simpson's style. So how would he take care of the guards? With the gas obviously, but how?

That question bothered Earp for some time into the night until a cigar-smoking player blew a gray cloud of smelly fumes in his face and he inadvertently coughed. Then he knew. Simpson had Patton's gas and he was planning to use it on the guards protecting the gold on the Flyer. But how? Simpson would be on the train, too. Wouldn't he be killed by the gas as well as the guards? Of course he would, unless he had a safe place on the train, a place where the gas couldn't reach him. But could he hide from the gas and still breathe air? That was a question for which he had no answer, so he turned his thinking to Hans Friedkin, Charlotte Simpson, and Horace Beal.

An odder threesome never existed. Earp could understand Friedkin and Charlotte being lovers, and he could comprehend Beal and Friedkin being anarchists. It was Charlotte's part that didn't make any sense. She was the daughter of a man of means, and coming from wealth, the fact that she embraced the lunatic fringe didn't add up. Maybe it was because she was in love with

Friedkin and espoused the cause for his sake. That had to be the reason. There seemed to be no other.

But what was this trio up to? So far, they had done nothing suspicious. Friedkin hadn't done anything that said he was still in the movement other than lead the miners against Simpson, and Charlotte and Beal weren't part of that. And what had they done? Nothing! That made him all the more suspicious. What were they up to?

As he closed down his game for the night, Earp still wondered about Beal, Friedkin, and Charlotte. It was close to daylight, and he was dog-tired. He and Big George were the only people left in the Dutchman's. Kramer was cleaning the last of the glasses as Earp counted his take for the night.

"Are you going over to Salome to see Roosevelt?" asked Earp, knowing full well that the mentioning of the former President's name would upset him.

"Might as well," said Kramer, surprising Earp by his casual response. "Won't be anyone around here until tonight. No sense in hanging around here by myself. What about you, Eagan? Are you going?"

"I don't know," said Earp. "It was a long night, and I'm beat in the ground. I'm going back to my hotel room for a long sleep, and I'll see about going over when I wake up. When is Roosevelt's train due in anyway?"

"Not until around two in the afternoon," said Kramer. "If you're going over, you'd better leave here by noon. How did you plan on getting there? The last stage leaves here at ten."

"I hadn't thought about that," said Earp.

"Maybe you should leave a wake-up call for nine-thirty or so. You do that, and I'll make sure they have a seat for you on the stage. How's that?"

"Sounds good to me, Big George. I'll do just that. Will you be taking the stage, too?"

"No, I'm riding my horse over to Salome. I want Colonel Roosevelt to see me on it."

"Colonel Roosevelt? Were you in the Rough Riders?" Earp already knew the answer, but he had to continue the charade.

"I was one of the first to volunteer," said Kramer. "I was with the colonel all the way through the war."

"Saw a lot of action, did you?"

Kramer blushed. "No, not really. Actually, I was a cook, but I was right there all the time. Napoleon said an army travels on its stomach, and I can vouch for that. Those boys sure ate everything I served up to them."

Earp finished counting, pocketed his share, and took Kramer's to him. "Here's yours, Big George. Good take tonight."

"Too bad we can't have more like it," said Kramer.

"Well, I'm turning in. I guess I'll see you in Salome."

"You bet. Now don't forget to leave that wake-up call."

"I won't."

Earp stepped outside just as the sun's first rays glowed over the eastern range of the Harqua Halas. The town was so quiet that it seemed almost ghostly. Slowly, he walked toward the Gold House.

TWENTY-THREE

Big George Kramer made doubly sure that Earp was out of bed by nine forty-five and getting ready to catch the stagecoach for Salome. He poured two cups of strong coffee into the former lawman, then walked him downstairs to the waiting conveyance. Still more than weary, Earp climbed aboard to join five other gentlemen inside the coach and three stop with the driver for the trip to Salome, and the stage departed on time.

The four horses pulling the vehicle slowed to a gait a bit slower than a trot at the first steep incline of the foothills. The right wheels bumped over a pothole, and the sharp jolt brought Earp fully awake, startling him into the realization that Big George seemed awfully eager to get him out of town. Kramer was a fairly nice man, but he wasn't that kind. Besides, he was one of Siringo's suspects in the murder of Walt Phillips. So why did he want Earp out of town? Only one way to find out.

Earp leaned out the window and shouted at the driver, "Stop the coach!"

"What's that?" shouted back the grizzled driver.

"I said, 'Stop the coach!' "

"Can't!"

"What do you mean, you can't?"

"Against company rules."

"Hang company rules!" yelled Earp angrily. "Stop this coach and now!"

"Can't!"

The driver's stubborn attitude irritated Earp. There was only one way to deal with a jackass. Earp sat back in his seat and drew his piece.

"Don't be alarmed, gents," he said to the other passengers. "I don't plan to harm anyone. I just want to get off this stagecoach before we get too far from Harqua Hala."

Satisfied that no one would interfere, he leaned out the window again and aimed the gun at the driver's head, and shouted once more, "Stop this stagecoach! And now!"

The driver, also irate, turned his head to shout over his right shoulder, saw the weapon, and changed his mind about telling Earp to sit down and shut up. Instead, he said, "Hey, what is this? A holdup?"

"No, you fool! I just want to get off."

"Get off? What the deuce for?"

"Never mind that! Do you stop now or do I start shooting?"

"Okay, okay," said the driver. "If you want off that bad, I'll stop at the top of the grade."

Earp understood and gave his approval.

As soon as the coach came to a halt, Earp climbed down, bidding the other passengers and the driver adieu.

"Now hold on a minute, friend," said the teamster. "Would you mind telling me why on earth you want to be let out here two miles from Harqua Hala and seven miles from Salome? Are you loco or something? You're too old to be wandering around the desert in this heat."

"Let's just say I'd rather walk than ride in that deathtrap," said Earp.

"Have it your way, then. Got any next of kin you want me to notify when you don't show up in town again?"

"Good idea. When you get to Salome, find Mr. Clayton Stewart and tell him Wade Eagan smelled a rat and went back to Harqua Hala to see if he couldn't catch him. You got that?"

"Mr. Clayton Stewart," said the driver. "Got it."

"And in case you can't find him, locate Sheriff Farnsworth and give him the same message."

"Sheriff Farnsworth? Hey, what's going on here?"

"Just do it, and there'll be something in it for you when I see you again."

"If you see me again, you mean," said the driver. "But don't worry. I'll give one of them your message. Whatever it is you're up to, Mr. Eagan, I wish you good luck."

"Thanks," said Earp. "Now get going."

The teamster slapped the reins on the horses backs, and the stagecoach pulled out.

It took Earp a good twenty minutes to get back to Harqua Hala. Instead of going back to the Gold House on Gold Street, he took

Salome Road past the cemetery, intending to go to the Dutchman's by way of Cemetery Street. As he walked by the graveyard, he saw Lester Higgins swinging a pick at the rocky hardpan as he dug a grave for the late Malcolm Caswell.

"Good day, Mr. Eagan," said Higgins, stopping his work. "What brings you out this way at this time of day?"

"Good day, Mr. Higgins," said Earp. "I might ask you why you're digging that grave in this heat."

"Heat?" queried Higgins, leaning on the pick. He removed his sombrero and wiped the sweat from his forehead with his shirt sleeve. "This ain't hot. Leastways, not as hot as where that banker has gone." He replaced the hat on his head.

"Is that so?" mused Earp.

"After what he and them others been doing, you can bet he's dancing down there at the end of the devil's pitchfork right now."

Earp's curiosity was piqued by the older man's remark. What had Higgins meant by that?

"Come again," said Earp.

"Don't you know? You ought to. Especially the way you and that Stewart fellow been nosing about since you hit town. And that young fellow Patton, too. What are you about anyway? You Pinkertons or something? I seen you, you know. Sneaking around at night, going up to Miss Sattin's room and talking for all hours, riding around in that young fellow's machine all over the place."

"You're a very observing fellow, aren't you, Mr. Higgins?"

"Dang tootin'! Ain't nothing goes on in Harqua Hala what I don't know about it. Why, I know more about every man, woman, and child in Harqua Hala than God Himself."

Earp chuckled at the boast, then said, "Then maybe you can tell me what happened to Mr. Patton. He's been missing since the night before last."

"Last I saw of him," said Higgins, "he was snooping around the newspaper office two nights ago."

"I know that," said Earp. "I saw him after that, but no one has seen him since."

"Well, I'll tell you this. I didn't see who it was, but I did see their tracks."

"Their tracks? What tracks?"

"They led from the back door of the newspaper office to the back door of the Dutchman's."

"What kind of tracks were they?"

"Two sets of men's boots with two straight lines running down between them."

Earp tried to envision the gravedigger's description, then voiced his conclusion. "Sounds to me like two men dragging a third. Is that what it looked like to you?"

"Hey, you're pretty smart, Mr. Eagan. That's exactly the way I saw it. Made me wonder if your friend Patton didn't go back there later and get himself conked on the noggin for snooping where he oughtn't have been snooping. But that don't explain why they dragged him over to the Dutchman's."

It did to Earp.

"I'll bet there's a lot you could tell me about all this," said Earp.

"All what?" queried Higgins. "I ain't quite figured out what you fellows are up to. Would you mind telling me about it?"

"Not at all, Mr. Higgins. We're trying to find out who killed Deputy Sheriff Walt Phillips."

"Is that all?"

"Well, it was until we started looking around," said Earp. "Now we think we've uncovered a plot to hold up the Flyer today."

"Is that a fact? Is that what Simpson's been up to these last few weeks? I was wondering about that. Him and that gunslinger Benteen been doing some mighty suspicious things of late. So that's what it's all about. Train holdup. They're going to do it today you say?"

"That's our guess. We figure they plan to stop the train at Granite Pass and take the gold there."

"That makes sense," said Higgins. "They've been digging over there for months. What do you suppose that's all about?"

"We haven't figured that out yet," said Earp. "What have you seen over there?"

"Not much. You can't get close to the place. Simpson's got armed men all over the place. But it must be a real big operation for them to need a railroad siding."

"A railroad siding? I don't understand."

"Well, they hauled in a bunch of ties and rails a couple weeks back," said Higgins. "If they ain't planning on building a siding, then what do they need those ties and rails for?"

Earp was stumped on that one, so he said, "A siding, I guess." Then he remembered why he had come back to Harqua Hala.

"You're sure about those tracks going from the back of the newspaper office to the back of the Dutchman's?"

"Positive," said Higgins. "You going to see if maybe your friend Patton is somewhere in the Dutchman's?"

"That's what I was thinking," said Earp. "I'll see you later, Mr. Higgins. I want to talk to you some more about Walt Phillips' murder."

"Any time," said Higgins. "Good luck finding your friend."

Earp walked down Cemetery Street toward the business district. He could see the jail at the corner of Main and Cemetery and wondered if he shouldn't get Jake Poole to help him search the Dutchman's for Patton. It was a good idea.

Poole was sleeping in his room when Earp entered the office. He came awake with the closing of the door and came out immediately in his stocking feet.

"Mr. Eagan, what are you doing here?"

"Looking for help, Jake," said Earp. "And you can stop calling me Mr. Eagan. My real name is Wyatt Earp, and I'm here as a special deputy for Sheriff Farnsworth."

"Wyatt Earp? You?"

"That's right, Jake."

"Well, I'll be. No wonder you were able to throw me that first day you came to town. You're Wyatt Earp."

"Never mind that now, Jake. Get your boots and gun on. I need you to back my play."

"Back your play? What—"

Earp lost his temper and snapped, "Get your boots on!"

Poole didn't hesitate this time. In less than a half minute, he was ready.

"We'll go out the back way," said Earp.

"Where are we going, Mr. Earp?" asked Poole as they exited the jailhouse.

"The Dutchman's. I have reason to believe George Patton is being held a prisoner there."

"Mr. Patton is a prisoner at the Dutchman's? What's going on here, Mr. Earp?"

"I haven't got time to explain, Jake," said Earp as they hurried up the alley. "Just be quiet now, and be ready to back me up if anyone tries to get in our way. You got that, Jake?"

"Yes, sir."

The back door to the Dutchman's was unlocked. Earp opened it slowly, and he and Poole went inside the short hallway that led to the barroom. There was one door on each side of the hall. The one to the left was Big George's living quarters, and the other was the storeroom. Earp bet on the latter and found it padlocked. He tried forcing it but was unsuccessful.

"Jake, come here," said Earp. He was obeyed. "Kick this door down. I think George is in here."

Poole obliged him by throwing his shoulder against the plank door. It gave way easily, the hasp breaking free of the frame, and the deputy stumbled into the dark room.

Earp stepped inside right after him, pushed Poole aside behind the door, and lit a match. He found the overhead lamp, pulled it down, lifted the lantern, and lit the wick. Upon lowering the glass, his eyes were drawn instantly to the far corner of the room where a gagged Patton was bound tightly to a wooden chair.

"George!" said Earp. He rushed over to Patton and removed the neckerchief from around his mouth. "George, are you all right, son?" He moved behind Patton and went to work on the ropes tied around the lieutenant's wrists.

". . . fine," rasped Patton.

"Did they hurt you, George?"

"No, I'm all right," said Patton. His hands came free, and he bent to remove the bindings around his ankles. "What day is it?"

"What day is it?" repeated Earp. "What kind of question is that?"

"I've lost all track of time," said Patton. "How long have I been in here?"

"It's Thursday," said Earp. "The last time I saw you was Tuesday night."

"Good Lord! What time is it?"

"It's too late for you," said Big George Kramer from the doorway, holding a double-barreled shotgun on them. He thumbed the hammers back one at a time and lifted the gun to his shoulder to draw aim on Patton and Earp.

Poole slammed the door on Kramer, knocking the shotgun away from its intended targets. Kramer's trigger finger tightened its grip, and the load of double-ought blasted into the end of a keg of beer, splintering the wood, the brew bursting forth in foamy streams.

Kramer reacted quickly, banging a forearm against the door, throwing it wide open again, and sprawling Poole to the floor.

Earp, standing now, went for his gun.

Patton, free from his bonds, leaped at Kramer.

Kramer didn't have time to train the gun on anyone. Going on instinct, he swung the barrels of the shotgun at Patton's head but struck the attacker's shoulder instead.

Patton glanced off the huge man and crashed into the door.

Poole scrambled to regain his feet.

Earp had his piece aimed at Kramer. "Hold it, Big George!"

Kramer ignored him and swung the shotgun around at Earp.

Earp fired. The .32-caliber slug tore into Kramer's meaty left shoulder, doing little more than rocking him back on his heels. He squeezed off another shot, this one hitting Kramer in the upper left chest and pushing him back against the doorjamb.

Patton got to his feet and jumped Kramer once more, achieving success as he crashed into the bleeding saloonkeeper and both men went down in a heap. The shotgun came free, skidding along the floor a few feet before coming to a rest out of Kramer's reach.

Earp and Poole moved in to help Patton. Earp kicked the shotgun farther away from Kramer, and Poole took aim at the big man with his Colt.

Kramer threw Patton off him as if he were a toy. Now a wounded, raging bull, he rolled over and tried to get up on his hands and knees. He never did.

Poole fired, shooting Kramer in the lower back. He started to pull the trigger again, but Earp knocked his gun aside.

"No, you damn fool!" shouted Earp. "Can't you see he's finished? There's no need to kill him!"

Kramer collapsed on the floor face down.

Patton got to one knee and prepared to leap on Kramer again if necessary. It wasn't.

Earp put his gun away and knelt down to see about Kramer's condition. He checked Kramer's breathing; it was deep and regular. He reached into his coat pocket, took out a handkerchief, and applied it to the wound in Kramer's back.

"Take it easy, Big George," said Earp. "Let us help you."

"You've killed me," said Kramer, "and now you want to help me. Don't make me laugh. Just let me die in peace."

"You aren't going to die yet," said Earp. "George, get me that neckerchief that was around your mouth."

Patton got it and handed it to Earp.

"Now help me turn him over on his back," said Earp. "You, too, Jake."

Poole holstered his piece and knelt to do his share of the work. With great effort, they rolled Kramer onto his back.

Earp applied the neckerchief to the chest wound and said, "Hold this in place, Big George. We can stop the bleeding."

"Why?" said Kramer. "I'm a dead man already."

"Not likely," said Earp. "How does your back feel?"

"How do you think it feels? It hurts."

"Where else does it hurt?" asked Earp.

"Where do you think it hurts? In my shoulder, you old fool!"

"How about your gut? Does that hurt, too?"

"Hell, no! You didn't shoot me there!"

"That's what I thought," said Earp. "You'll live all right."

"Well, I don't want to live just to get hanged. Shoot me again and let me die."

"Why would anyone want to hang you?" asked Earp. "Would it be because you killed Walt Phillips?"

"Walt Phillips? What the hell are you talking about, Eagan? Or is that your real name?"

"This is Wyatt Earp," said Poole.

"So you are Wyatt Earp after all," said Kramer. "That's what old man Higgins called you, and we didn't believe it."

"Good Lord, Wyatt!" said Patton. "In all the excitement, I forgot about Roosevelt."

"What's this, George?"

"President Roosevelt," said Patton. "Friedkin and Beal are planning to blow up his train after it leaves Salome."

"Why on earth didn't you say so sooner? He'll be in Salome in less than three hours. We've got to hurry and get there and alert Clyde Farnsworth."

TWENTY-FOUR

The Flyer left Phoenix at eleven that morning consisting of a 4-4-0 coal-fired Baldwin locomotive, coal tender, mail car, baggage car, a Pullman, and two coaches. Its schedule included a fifteen-minute stop in Wickenburg and another in Parker. Although it left the capital three hours later, the Flyer would pass through Salome while Roosevelt's campaign train sat at the stockyard siding.

Aware of the Flyer's schedule, Siringo and Farnsworth sat up much of the night discussing the situation. They reasoned that Simpson had probably booked a sleeping compartment on the Pullman for himself and Kilpatrick in order to place themselves as close to the baggage and mail cars as possible. Because he was one of the mine owners whose gold was being shipped to the mint, Simpson had most likely been given access to both cars. Somehow, he and Kilpatrick would then get the drop on the guards and disarm them. Then it would only be a small matter of stopping the train and removing the gold. A very simple plan.

Siringo and Farnsworth were faced with the problem of thwarting Simpson in the act without anyone getting hurt. Therein lay the rub. They worked on several possible solutions, but none of them totally precluded the probability that someone would be injured. Finally accepting this as fact, they went to bed with a plan.

Everything was set in place for springing the trap on Simpson until Earp and Patton rolled into Salome shortly after noon in Patton's Hupmobile. Immediately, they sought out Siringo and Farnsworth at Sheffler's.

"They're gone," said Sheffler. "They rode out before sunup, leading a posse."

"Which way did they go?" asked Earp.

"West."

Earp turned to Patton and said, "They've probably gone out to stop Simpson."

"George!" called a familiar voice.

Patton turned around to see Captain William Mitchell standing in the doorway, his hands on the hips of cavalry riding trousers.

Forgetting the moment, Patton hurried over to greet his old friend. "Billy! How'd you get here?"

Shaking hands vigorously, Mitchell replied, "I flew here."

"Flew?"

"That's right. In my aeroplane."

"Oh, yes, I heard about that. But what are you doing here?"

"I came to see you and deliver a message."

"A message?"

Mitchell glanced around the crowded room, then said, "George, we'd better talk in private."

Patton understood. "Sure. But first I want you to meet someone." He led Mitchell over to Earp. "Billy, this is Mr. Wyatt Earp."

Mitchell was astounded. "Wyatt Earp?"

Several men overheard the introduction and reacted the same as Mitchell, and almost instantly, the famous gunfighter's name was on everyone's lips as the saloon buzzed with excitement.

Earp was embarrassed by the sudden attention. He shook hands with Mitchell, then turned to Sheffler and asked, "Have you got a private room where we can talk?"

"Sure thing, Mr. Earp," said Sheffler, who was as excited as the rest. "Right this way." He headed toward the rear of the saloon, walking behind the bar, as Earp, Patton, and Mitchell followed, working their way through the crowd. Sheffler opened the door to the back room for them and asked, "Is there anything I can get you, Mr. Earp? On the house?"

"A couple of iced beers for George and me," said Earp. "How about you, Captain? Would you like something to drink?"

"Iced beer sounds good to me," said Mitchell.

Sheffler left, closing the door behind him.

"Okay, Billy," said Patton, "what's this message you have for me?" He noticed how Mitchell seemed leery of speaking in front of Earp. "Wyatt knows everything, Billy, if this message has anything to do with why I'm here. You can talk in front of him."

"Okay, if you say so," said Mitchell. "Colonel Hardesty said to tell you that two masks were discovered missing."

Before anyone could respond, Sheffler returned with frosty

mugs of foamy, cold beer. He set them down on the table, then left them alone again.

Patton seemed puzzled at first about Hardesty's message. Then, as if someone had just drawn the drapes of his brain and let the sunshine in, he understood.

Not so Earp as he asked, "Masks?"

"Gas masks," said Patton. "It's a breathing device you wear over your face to protect you from poisonous gas. I'm not sure how it works, but if Simpson has those masks, he can release the gas anytime he wants and be safe."

"And everyone around him will be killed," said Earp. "Is that it, George?"

"That's right!"

"And Charlie and Clyde are out there with a posse."

"And they'll all be killed if Simpson explodes that canister. Wyatt, we've got to get them out of there."

"What are you two talking about?" asked Mitchell.

"You might as well know, too, Billy," said Patton. "Wyatt and Mr. Charles Siringo came here to investigate the murder of a deputy sheriff, and I came here looking for a canister of phosgene gas that was stolen from Fort Huachuca. As fantastic as this may sound, Billy, we've uncovered a plot to rob a train and another plot to kill President Roosevelt."

"Assassinate Roosevelt?"

"That's right," said Earp. "And now we're pretty sure that a man named Simpson has the gas and is planning to use it to rob the train."

"I don't understand about this gas," said Mitchell. "What's so important about it?"

"Billy, phosgene is chlorine gas, and it's very lethal," said Patton, choosing to speak in terms Mitchell would understand better. "One canister can wipe out a battalion of soldiers."

Mitchell let out a low whistle, then said, "This could change warfare forever."

"That's right," said Patton. "Load up a single canister in a howitzer and shoot it into the middle of an attacking army, and you can get instant victory."

"But what about this plot to kill Roosevelt?" asked Mitchell. "What about that?"

"A small group of anarchists are planning to blow up the railroad tracks when Roosevelt's campaign train passes over them," said Patton. "The only trouble is, we don't know exactly where they plan to do it. All we have to go by is my shaky memory of a map I saw two nights ago for less than two minutes."

"What are you going to do?" asked Mitchell.

"Good question," said Earp. "I think the first thing we'd better do is find out when those two trains are due to arrive here in Salome. Then we'll know how much time we have to act and on which one we should act first."

"Well, I can help you some there," said Mitchell. "President Roosevelt's train is due here at two o'clock."

"What about the Flyer?" asked Earp.

"Sorry," said Mitchell. "I can't help you there."

"Then we'd better go over to the station and find out about the Flyer," said Patton.

They drank up and left through the back door. Two minutes later they were at the depot, questioning the stationmaster.

"The Flyer?" asked the stationmaster. "It left Phoenix two hours ahead of schedule because of Roosevelt's train." He checked his pocket watch. "Ought to come through here any minute now."

"Any minute?" exclaimed an alarmed Earp. "We don't have any time left, George. We'd better get in your automobile and get to Granite Pass now."

The lonesome call of a train whistle howled in the distance, signaling impending doom.

"Good Lord!" said Patton. "We're too late!"

"What's wrong?" asked Mitchell anxiously.

"Everything," said Earp. "The Flyer will be coming through here in a minute or two, and Charlie and the posse are over at Granite Pass. We can't get there in time to warn them about the gas."

"Wait! We can stop the train here!" said Patton.

"No, we can't," said Earp. "If Simpson has the gas on the train and he panics, he could kill a lot of innocent people. No, we have to let the Flyer pass through here, then stop it somewhere out in the open. Before it gets to Granite Pass."

The train whistle sounded again, closer this time.

"Then what are we waiting for?" said Patton.

"You'll never make it in time in an automobile," said Mitchell.

"We don't have any other choice," said Patton.

"Yes, we do," said Mitchell. "We can take my aeroplane. I can fly you to Granite Pass."

"What's this?" asked Earp. "Fly us there?"

"Well, not both of you," said Mitchell. "But I could fly one of you there."

Earp and Patton looked at each other, wondering which of them would take up the challenge.

"I'd better do it," said Patton. "I'm . . . uh—"

"Younger, George?" said Earp. "You're right. I am too old for this sort of thing. You go with Captain Mitchell, and I'll take your automobile."

"But you don't know how to drive a car, Wyatt," said Patton.

"If you can get in that aeroplane with Captain Mitchell," said Earp, "then I can drive a car."

The Flyer cried out again, and all three looked east to see the train approaching, its stack spewing an ominous black cloud that trailed behind it.

"Get going, George," said Earp. "There's not another minute to lose."

Patton and Mitchell sprinted across the road to the waiting aeroplane.

"George, you'll have to spin the prop for me," said Mitchell.

"Do what?"

"The propeller, George. I'll get in and turn on the switch. When I say 'Contact!' you spin the propeller. Got it?"

"Got it," said Patton.

Mitchell climbed into the cockpit, switched on the magneto, and yelled out, "Contact!"

Patton spun the propeller, and the engine sputtered and coughed. They repeated the process, and the motor caught and roared.

Patton ran around the wing to the cockpit. "Where do I sit?" he asked.

"You don't," shouted Mitchell over the Martin's whining engine. "You have to lie on the wing."

Patton looked at the wing in disbelief. Then in the distance he saw the Flyer race through Salome. The wing it would be. He lowered the driving goggles over his eyes, removed his duster and threw it aside, then lay down on the wing and took hold of the closest strut and a guy wire.

"Be careful not to tear the fabric," said Mitchell.

"Got it," said Patton.

"Okay, hold on. Here we go."

Mitchell released the brake, and the Martin "T" jerked forward, then began to roll. It bumped into the road, and Mitchell turned it into the west wind. He increased the throttle, and the aeroplane began to pick up speed as it taxied past Sheffler's, scattering those who remained in the street. Through the town, faster and faster, the craft roared ahead. Then past the last building, Mitchell pulled back on the stick gently, and the Martin was no longer earth-bound. Up it rose, the wind whipping Patton's face. Five feet, ten feet, then above the tops of the telegraph poles it climbed. Higher and higher went the aeroplane until it attained an altitude of a hundred feet, and with each passing second, it gained on the Flyer racing along the tracks below.

"That's Granite Pass up there," said Patton, motioning with his head.

Mitchell looked toward the cut between the mountains, then scanned the railroad line. Quickly, he summed up the odds of getting to the pass ahead of the train, finding a place to set down, landing, and seeking out Siringo and the posse. They weren't good, figuring they had two chances: slim and none.

"George, we can't make it. There isn't enough time."

"What do we do now?" asked Patton.

"You tell me."

Now they had caught up with the train and were directly over it. An idea came to Patton.

"Land on the train, Billy."

"What? Are you crazy?" asked Mitchell. "I can't do that."

"Then get low enough so I can drop down on top of it."

"You are crazy, George. You'll be killed."

"I have to try it, Billy. I've got to stop Simpson from exploding that canister of gas. Get me down there, Billy."

"I still say you're crazy," said Mitchell, "but I'll get you down there."

Mitchell eased the stick forward and cut back on the throttle to slow the Martin to the same speed as the train. Now, directly over the tender, the aeroplane began a gentle descent. In a few seconds, they were smelling the fumes of the coal-burning locomotive, causing Mitchell to decelerate even more, the aircraft falling back car by car. As the last coach crept beneath them, the Martin was less than ten feet above it.

Patton let go of the strut and took hold of another guy wire, allowing himself to slide backward until his legs dangled off the wing.

"Put your feet on the carriage axle," said Mitchell. "Then take my hand." He held out his hand for emphasis.

Patton got the idea. His feet found the bar between the wheels, then he stretched out his right hand and took Mitchell's grip.

"Now reach down and grab the landing strut with your other hand," said Mitchell.

Patton did, but in doing so, his feet slipped off the axle and he lost hold of Mitchell's hand, leaving him hanging by his weaker hand. Quickly, he grabbed the axle with his right and hung there for an instant before falling to the roof of the coach, landing face down. He slid to one side, nearly going over it until he caught hold of two ventilation pipes, one with a foot. Pulling himself back onto the raised center part of the roof, he had the presence of mind to look up and wave to Mitchell and let him know that he was safe for the moment.

TWENTY-FIVE

Realizing that he had plenty of time before Roosevelt's train was due in Salome and that there was little he could do about Siringo, Farnsworth, and the posse, not to mention Patton and Mitchell, Earp decided he should do something about Friedkin and Beal.

While helping Jake Poole get Big George Kramer into a jail cell and giving the wounded saloonkeeper additional medical attention, Earp learned that Friedkin and Beal were planning to set dynamite charges along the railroad tracks, either between Wenden and Salome or between Salome and Granite Pass, at one of the bridges over the many arroyos the road passed over. Kramer bragged that there was nothing they could do to stop Friedkin and Beal because they had set several charges along the line the day before and that by the time Roosevelt came to town both Friedkin and Beal would be nowhere to be found. Earp didn't believe him. No self-respecting criminal, whether he was an anarchist or whatever, wouldn't want to be around when the crime was set to come off.

Strangely enough, Kramer made no mention of Charlotte Simpson and her role in the assassination plot. Earp questioned him about her, but Kramer ignored him. However, Patton mentioned during the ride to Salome how she had been quite aggressive when he was spying on the anarchists before the storm two nights previous. This, added to what Earp had heard her say the day of the street fight between Jake Poole and Friedkin, convinced Earp that Charlotte was no mere starry-eyed schoolgirl in love with a fanatic; she was a fanatic herself.

Figuring that Roosevelt's train would be coming from the east, Earp decided the best place to start looking for trouble was between Wenden and Salome. He climbed into the Hupmobile and checked over the controls—steering wheel, hand brake, clutch, gas pedal, gearshift, magneto switch. It didn't seem very complicated; just a matter of pushing, pulling, or turning the right one at the right time. All he needed was someone to turn the crank, and for that, he had plenty of volunteers.

Wickenburg Road paralleled the rails all the way to Wenden, the distance separating the two being less than fifty feet. Whereas the railroad bed bridged every wash and arroyo in its path, the highway followed the natural contour of the land, dipping wherever slashing torrents of rainwater scarred the desert floor. The recent showers had carved even deeper into the land, making the roadway bumpier than usual.

Earp had covered half of the five miles to Wenden and looked under two dozen bridges when it dawned on him that Friedkin and Beal weren't so foolish that they would set charges under bridges that could be seen from the road. Of course not. They would most likely choose a spot that couldn't be observed very well, and the only place that fit that description was in the foothills of the Harcuvar Mountains, within two miles of Granite Pass and adjacent to Walt Phillips' mining claims.

He turned the car around and headed back to Salome at full speed.

TWENTY-SIX

After his and Patton's experience at Granite Pass earlier in the week, Siringo thought it might be best if the posse approached it from a different direction, one in which Simpson's men might not be looking. So he and Farnsworth led the deputies in a circuitous route that took them west along the tracks for a mile, then north until they reached the Harcuvar Mountains. They worked in and out of the foothills until they reached the low ridges above the first curve in the railroad. By then, it was nearly ten o'clock. Siringo split them into two groups, one led by himself and the other by Farnsworth. The sheriff took his bunch over the hills to the Bouse Valley side. Then both parties dismounted and went the rest of the way on foot. By noon, they were all in positions above the outlaw camp.

Siringo had had the forethought to bring along a pair of field glasses. At half past noon, he scanned the area from his vantage point above Simpson's men.

The outlaw camp was strategically placed in a hollow between two ridges. Six tents were pitched around the adit of a mine shaft, over which stood an A-frame for block and tackle. The upper end of the canyon was fenced off for a corral, and Siringo counted twenty-four horses in it. At the lower end, six men—divided into pairs—stood guard, each man with a rifle and six-shooter. One set watched the pass; another the road and tracks to the west; and the third the road and tracks to the east. Six more men were gathered around a picnic table in the center of everything; they were drinking and playing cards. That made twelve outlaws. Siringo figured the other twelve were either down in the shaft or in the tents; or each man had two horses. One of the former possibilities was most likely because the number of men he had seen in Harqua Hala tallied with the information given him by both Mamie Sattin and Al Ziegler.

Although their numbers were nearly equal, Siringo considered the posse to have the advantages of surprise and control of higher ground. If a shoot-out should become necessary, he felt confident that the outcome would be in their favor. With the situation and the opposition sized up, there seemed to be little else to do but wait for the Flyer to come around the first bend in the tracks.

It was a short wait.

Although the Flyer was a good five miles away, the lonesome wail of its steam whistle was easy to recognize. Siringo turned his binoculars in the direction of Salome, and sure enough, he saw the black billows of coal smoke rising above the train as it roared through the town. As he watched it come on, he noticed in the corner of his view that Mitchell's biplane was taking off from the road. Distracted by the aeroplane and with great curiosity, he followed the air machine's flight as it banked slightly to its right, then leveled off over the onrushing train. His fascination with the Martin "T" grew with each passing second until he saw Patton dangling from the landing carriage.

"Good heavens!" he muttered unwittingly and totally absorbed in the excitement of the scene unfolding before him. "What's he doing? Is he crazy?"

Then he saw Patton fall to the roof of the last coach, scramble about, right himself, and signal to Mitchell. The Martin then gained altitude, passed the train below it, and flew over Siringo and the posse scattered in the foothills. Without the aid of the glasses, he watched it circle above Granite Pass once, then head back toward Salome.

Siringo's attention was then drawn to Patton atop the train. As the Flyer entered the first curve in the line, it was slowed by the uphill grade and the bend in the tracks. Patton worked his way forward on the roofs of the cars. By the second curve, he had reached the baggage car; by the third, the mail car. Siringo lost sight of the train in the fourth and last bend, which led into the tunnel.

He turned the binoculars on the outlaw camp and saw that the guards had come down from their posts and had gathered around the shaft with the men who had been at the picnic table. More outlaws climbed out of the hole. One man began pointing and shouting, obviously giving orders as several of them began running in different directions at the same time. Two villains disappeared into a tent, then reappeared within seconds carrying a large tube-shaped object that had—

"Great God in heaven!" mouthed Siringo. "That's it!"

The time had come for action.

TWENTY-SEVEN

Mitchell flew his Martin "T" a mile past Salome, intending to come around and land into the wind on the road just east of the town. Looking down the length of Wickenburg Road, he saw Earp in the Hupmobile, speeding toward Salome, and in the distance he saw the black plumes of coal smoke generated by Roosevelt's train. Quickly, he estimated the former President would be arriving in Salome in less than ten minutes, and it struck him that time was running out on them.

Then disaster struck.

Mitchell banked the aeroplane to bring it around for the landing. Looking down, he saw the Hupmobile suddenly twist sideways in the sandy bottom of a wash, hit the embankment on the far side of the gully, and flip over, throwing the driver clear of the wreck. Instead of leveling out, Mitchell kept the craft in its arcing pattern, circling over the automobile. His heart skipped several beats when he ascertained that Earp wasn't moving.

"My God! I've got to get down there!"

He thought about putting down right there, but realizing the road was too rough along that stretch, he chose to return to Salome.

Mitchell landed his aeroplane in the road and taxied it to the same spot where he had parked before. He jumped down from the cockpit and ran into the street just as dozens of people surrounded him, all talking about the flying machine and its operator. Fathers told their sons how fortunate they were to be born in such a magnificent age; sons questioned their fathers about the mechanics of internal-combustion engines and the principles of flight. Women whispered to each other about the dashing appearance of the pilot. Almost everyone seemed to have lost contact with the reason they were there.

All but Mitchell.

"Quiet down!" he shouted at the crowd. "Quiet down!"

Like ripples in a pond, silence spread through the throng, giving Mitchell command.

"There's been an accident down the road," said Mitchell, "and Mr. Earp is hurt."

Before he could give them any details, a train whistle announced Roosevelt's impending arrival.

"He's coming!" shouted someone.

"It's Roosevelt's train!" yelled another.

Within seconds, the crowd forgot about Mitchell and began moving en masse toward the depot.

"Wait!" shouted Mitchell. "I need help. Mr. Earp is hurt, and I need someone to go with me to help him."

Everyone ignored him.

Mitchell couldn't believe it, but he didn't have time to ponder the apathy of this mindless mob. Earp was hurt and needed aid. He had to act and promptly.

Several saddled horses were tied up at the hitching rail in front of the train depot. Being a fair judge of horseflesh, Mitchell ran over to them and picked out a good one. He threw himself onto the back of a white-faced roan, jerked the reins, and charged off down the road. The owner of the animal, even if he saw Mitchell take his property, made no protest.

Roosevelt's train was less than a mile away when Mitchell passed it going east. Ahead of him, he saw the Hupmobile on its side, blocking the road, its tires still spinning; but he couldn't see Earp. The injured man must still be in the gully.

He was, lying motionless, face down in the sand, appearing to be a human pretzel.

Mitchell rode right up to Earp and jumped down before the horse had come to a full halt, the momentum of the maneuver carrying him past the accident victim. He slipped and fell as he tried to stop himself suddenly. He scrambled on his hands and knees to get to Earp.

"Mr. Earp! Mr. Earp! Are you all right?" Mitchell realized that was a stupid question, so he began checking the man's injuries.

Earp was unconscious but was still breathing steadily. Other than a few minor abrasions on his face, there was no serious bleeding. Broken bones? How could one tell? Feel his limbs? Mitchell started with Earp's legs; both seemed to be intact. The arms? Okay. Collarbones? Both sound. The ribs?

Before Mitchell could check the rib cage, Earp groaned.

"Mr. Earp, are you all right? Can you hear me? Are you all right?"

Earp groaned again, and his hands instinctively reached for his head.

"Mr. Earp, can you hear me? It's me. Billy Mitchell. Can you hear me?"

"Captain Mitchell," said Earp slowly. "What happened? Never mind. I remember now." He pushed himself up on one elbow and felt his skinned forehead with his free hand. "Took a nasty turn for the worse back there, didn't I? Man, does my head hurt!"

"Do you hurt anywhere else?" asked Mitchell.

"Everything seems to be in working order," said Earp, "but I can tell you this. I don't think there's a place on my whole body that doesn't hurt." He pushed himself up on the other elbow. "Help me up, Captain."

Slowly and carefully, Mitchell assisted Earp to his feet.

The legendary gunfighter looked at the damaged Hupmobile and said, "Those things are killers."

"The price of progress," said Mitchell matter-of-factly.

Suddenly, Earp was attuned to the current problem again. "Where's George? Is he all right?"

"I put him down on the train," said Mitchell.

"On the train?"

"I'll tell you about it later," said Mitchell. "Right now, we've got a bigger problem. Roosevelt's train just arrived in Salome."

"Good Lord, man! We've got to get back there and stop him from leaving until we find those anarchists."

Mitchell looked around for the horse he had borrowed. He saw it trotting down the road toward Salome.

TWENTY-EIGHT

Patton saw the tunnel ahead. He cursed himself for being so slow; he had only reached the mail car.

The grade and the curves in the line had slowed the Flyer from a powerful forty-five miles per hour to a mere fifteen as the locomotive entered the tunnel. To the train crew, this trip seemed like any other; load up the gold and the two dozen armed guards in Phoenix, then race to San Francisco. The change in departure time had affected no one other than a few potential passengers who didn't get the word soon enough to change their plans and make the train. For the engine team, the fact that there were only a handful of people on board with their luggage made a lighter load and thus an easier job for them.

Patton saw the light at the other end of the tunnel at the same time as the engineer, but unlike the man at the throttle, Patton knew there was trouble inside the long shaft. He made the jump from the mail car onto the coal tender amid a dense rush of choking black smoke and the deafening roar of the train reverberating off the granite walls of the passageway. He crawled forward on the chunks of coal, then suddenly he fell sideways as the train lurched to the left. Clinging to the side of the car, he looked up to see the end of the tunnel. But he shouldn't have been able to see it; the engine should have blocked his view. Where was the locomotive?

The engineer was wondering the same thing. Startled by the unexpected turn of the tracks into a torch-lit side tunnel, he reached for the controls, easing off on the throttle at first, then shifting into reverse, the best method of braking. Steel wheels on steel tracks screeched eerily, and sparks flashed in ghastly profusion, making ghoulish specters of the crew and Patton. But the action availed nothing. Although the train slowed and came to a near halt, it continued to slide forward against its iron drive, being pulled ahead by the gravity of a decline in the road. Then a heavy jolt shuddered through the entire train as the locomotive made an unscheduled stop at the end of the uncharted siding.

Patton was thrown forward into the cab, colliding with the fireman and bumping against the engineer. The fireman caught the newcomer, and both men went down. As they regained their feet, the engineer disengaged the controls.

"Great Scot!" yelled the engineer. "Where did you come from, man?"

"Never mind that now!" snapped Patton as he scrambled to his feet. "We've got to get everyone out of here as fast as we can! We're all in grave danger! There's a man on this train who has a deadly gas, and he's planning to kill everyone with it!"

"What in heaven's name are you talking about, man?" asked the engineer.

Patton pulled out his Pocket .38 and said, "There's no time for explanations now. Just get moving out of here."

"But which way do we go?" asked the fireman.

Patton jumped down, then said, "Back where we came in. Just get out of here now, and get everyone to go with you. Get those men out of the cars and get as far away from here as you can as fast as you can."

"What is this?" demanded the engineer. "A holdup?"

"That's right," said Patton as he looked toward the rear of the train. He saw several men near the baggage car.

"That's just what I thought," said the engineer.

Patton looked up to see the man holding a gun on him. "Not me, you fool! The bandits are down there!" He pointed with his Smith & Wesson.

The sound of gunfire echoed from somewhere outside the tunnel, and Patton ducked instinctively. Fortunately for him it happened just then, because at that very second the engineer pulled the trigger on his piece, and the bullet narrowly missed Patton's head.

"What the hell are you doing?" yelled Patton, looking back at the engineer. Then seeing the man taking aim for a second shot, he jumped under the train.

The engineer leaped from the cab in pursuit, but luck wasn't with him. He hit the ground in time to catch a rifle slug intended for Patton. It caught him in the shoulder and knocked him to the dirt.

Patton expected a small war to break out in the tunnel, but the only gunfire seemed to be coming from and going to the outside. Where were the guards? Why weren't they shooting? Then it hit him. Simpson and Kilpatrick had disarmed the guards! Or had they? Maybe they had the guards locked inside the mail and baggage cars where they couldn't interfere with what was happening in the tunnel. That had to be it. He had to get to the mail car and free the guards.

As Patton crawled along the makeshift tracks, he heard Ardmore Simpson shouting at his men.

"What's wrong here, Shonsey?" he demanded.

"There's a posse up there," said the henchman.

"A posse?" queried Simpson. "Where did they come from?"

"I don't know, Mr. Simpson, but there has to be twenty or thirty men up there with rifles."

"Twenty or thirty men? Are you sure?"

"Well, I didn't stop to count them," said Shonsey, "but I know there's a whole hell of a lot of them up there."

"All right," said Simpson. "Get everyone down in the tunnel. We'll go out the other way. Where's the gas?"

"It's right here, Mr. Simpson."

"Kilpatrick, get the masks," said Simpson. "Shonsey, get the boys out of here. Kilpatrick and I will take care of the gas."

"All right, you heard the man!" shouted Shonsey. "Let's get the hell out!"

Patton saw the boots and legs of several men as they ran toward the main tunnel. The shooting outside ceased. Then he saw Simpson kneeling beside the canister of gas.

"What's going on here?" someone shouted at the other end of the train.

A single gunshot rang out, followed by a death scream. Then a woman shrieked.

The passengers! thought Patton. But they weren't his concern right now. He had to stop Simpson from exploding the gas. He took aim at the outlaw and fired and missed, the bullet ricocheting off the rocks behind Simpson.

Simpson jumped behind a granite protrusion. "Kilpatrick, where are you?"

"Back here," said Kilpatrick. "Take it easy, boss. I'll get him."

Patton heard the click of a .44's hammer.

"Throw me a mask," said Simpson.

Kilpatrick obliged him.

Patton saw Kilpatrick's boots at the other end of the car. He took aim and fired and hit the gunfighter just above the left ankle.

Kilpatrick yelped, then hopped backward on one foot. "Sonofa-bitch! You'll pay for that!"

Patton lost sight of Kilpatrick's feet. He looked toward Simpson and saw the mine owner reaching for the canister. He shot at Simpson's hand and missed again, but he did force Simpson to withdraw.

"Hurry up and kill him, Kilpatrick!" shouted Simpson.

There was no answer, and that worried Patton. Kilpatrick was on the move. The question was where.

Patton rolled out from under the tracks, stood up, and began working his way back to the engine. The locomotive was still huffing and hissing, and the sounds covered the noises of Patton's feet. He found the engineer sitting on the ground, leaning against the last wheel, holding his wounded shoulder. The fireman was still in the cab, cringing with fear. Patton saw the engineer's gun, a Smith & Wesson Schofield .45, and picked it up. The .45 was a far better weapon than his Pocket .32.

"Are you all right?" asked Patton.

"I'll live," said the engineer, "but you sure look a sight."

Patton didn't understand that the engineer was referring to his sooted face and clothes. From head to toe, he was almost totally black.

"Who's that?" whispered the fireman.

Patton looked at him, then shifted his eyes in the direction the fireman was staring.

A shot rang out. The fireman fell dead.

Kilpatrick lay prone atop the mail car, his gun arm extended. He was looking for another target, but from the expression on his face, he couldn't see anyone, not even Patton, who was sure he was a dead man.

Realizing his advantage, Patton took slow deliberate aim with the Schofield. He fired once.

Kilpatrick lurched upward, then crumpled back on the roof. His .44 dropped from his hand. He was dead.

Now to stop Simpson.

Patton hurried toward the mail car. When he reached the coupling between it and the tender, he crossed to the other side of the tracks and saw Simpson with his back to him bent over the canister.

"Hold it right there, Simpson!" ordered Patton.

Simpson straightened up and spun around. He was wearing a gas mask and holding a stick of dynamite with a burning fuse.

What to do? Patton was undecided. Shoot Simpson? Run? What? He knew he had to do something. But what?

Simpson made the decision for him. He tossed the dynamite at Patton, then ran toward the main tunnel.

Patton's first reaction was to duck, the TNT landing at his feet. Regaining control, he dropped the gun, and grabbed the explosive. Thinking fast, he ripped out the fuse and threw it away. Then he saw the flame on the canister of phosgene. It was fifty feet away. There was no time, but he had to try. He broke into a run, tripped, fell, and bumped his head against the rock wall, sending his senses into a spin. He was out of time.

Upon seeing Patton on the train and spotting what had to be the canister of phosgene in the outlaw camp, Siringo ordered the posse to open fire in hopes that they would drive the outlaws down the shaft and thus disrupt their plan. They succeeded.

In an instant, Siringo deduced that the opening he could see had to lead to a branch tunnel from the railroad passageway. That conclusion was confirmed when the train failed to exit the tunnel on the other side of the mountain and when he saw black smoke rising from the shaft. Therefore, Siringo called out to Farnsworth to take his men and cover both ends of the railroad tunnel. Siringo then led his group down the hill to the outlaw camp, approaching the adit with caution.

A gunshot reverberated up from the tunnel. Patton! thought Siringo. He looked down the hole but saw nothing other than the ladder. Gun in hand, he started down the ladder. As he reached the third-from-last rung, he heard Patton call out to Simpson. He took the final three steps to the bottom. Simpson was gone, but the canister wasn't. He went to it immediately and extinguished the burning dynamite fuses.

"Charlie!" called Patton, holding his head and struggling to rise. "The gas! Put out the—"

"It's all right, George. I already took care of it. Where's Simpson?"

Patton got to his feet and stumbled toward Siringo. "He ran toward the railroad tunnel," said Patton.

"Then it's all right," said Siringo. "Farnsworth and the boys will get him along with the others. Come on. Let's see about the guards on the train."

More deputies came down the ladder, and Siringo and Patton unlocked the baggage and mail cars, adding the railroad guards to their force. Within a quarter hour, they had Simpson and his gang under arrest.

TWENTY-NINE

Fortunately, Earp wasn't hurt seriously; bumps, bruises, and abrasions, but nothing broken.

With the horse run off, Mitchell sized up their situation instantly. It was either hoof it to Salome or try to upright the Hupmobile, get it started, and drive back. The auto was light enough to accomplish the feat, and although Earp ached terribly, he and Mitchell pushed the car back onto its wheels. Mitchell turned the crank, but the engine failed to respond. He tried again. Still nothing. A third attempt. No good.

"There's something damaged," said Mitchell. "I'll have a look at the motor." He lifted the left panel and examined the engine. "Here's the trouble. Disconnected wires." He made the connections, then cranked the motor again. Still nothing. "It must be something else."

"The smell of gasoline is heavy about us, Captain," said Earp. "Could the fuel tank be empty?"

"Possibly," said Mitchell. "I'll check it." He did. "No, the gasoline tank is all right, and there is gasoline in it. I'll check the motor again." He looked again but could find nothing out of order. "I don't understand it. It seems to be okay, but it doesn't turn over."

"Well, we'd better start walking," said Earp. "Time is wasting."

"I suppose you're right. Better switch off the magneto. There's no sense in running down the battery."

"Turn off the what?" queried Earp.

"The magneto," said Mitchell. Then he understood. "Didn't you turn on the magneto?"

"You mean this thing?"

"No wonder it wouldn't start. Turn it on, and I'll give it another go."

Earp did his part, and Mitchell did his. The engine chugged and started, and they were on their way toward town.

Over five hundred people formed a human half-circle at the end of Roosevelt's train, listening to the former President give yet another campaign speech. Everyone ignored Mitchell and Earp as they returned to Salome.

"We've got to keep that train here," said Earp, "until we make sure it's safe. Drive around the crowd to the engine, and we'll talk to the engineer."

Mitchell complied, and in a minute he parked the Hupmobile beside the locomotive. A youthful gentleman, smartly dressed in a light gray suit, approached them.

"You can't be here," he said, shaking a hand at Earp and Mitchell. "You'll have to move back with the rest of the folks."

"Who are you?" asked Earp.

"Never mind who I am. Just do as you're told."

"Are you one of Mr. Roosevelt's guards?"

"That's right. Now move along."

"Good," said Earp. "We need to talk to you right away. Mr. Roosevelt's life is in danger."

"What's this?" queried the guard, reaching inside his coat for his gun.

"Not here," said Earp. "Down the tracks." He pointed west. "There are some fanatics up ahead who are planning to blow up the train."

"How do you know that?" asked the guard.

"This is Wyatt Earp," said Mitchell as if that should explain everything.

"Wyatt Earp? This old man?"

"Believe me, pal. This is Wyatt Earp, and he's telling you the truth."

"And who are you?" asked the guard.

"Captain William Mitchell, United States Army."

"Look, friend," said Earp, "there's no time for discussion. Those anarchists are planning to blow up this train when it crosses a bridge up in those hills. You've got to warn Mr. Roosevelt and keep him here until we round up those criminals and make sure it's safe for Mr. Roosevelt to continue his trip."

"That's impossible," said the guard. "The colonel will be through speaking any minute now, and he won't want to be late for his next engagement in Parker."

"If you don't keep him here until we do something about those anarchists," said Earp, "he'll never get to Parker for that speech."

The guard studied their faces for a moment, then said, "Wait here. I'll have to tell the boss." He turned and walked toward the rear of the train.

"Do you think he believed us?" asked Mitchell.

"I have my doubts," said Earp. "We'd better not wait. The sooner we get to Friedkin and Beal, the sooner it will be safe for Mr. Roosevelt to travel."

"I agree. So what do you want me to do, Mr. Earp?"

"Good question, Captain. We've only got one gun between us, and out in the open, my .32 won't be much help. I wish we had a couple of rifles."

Mitchell scanned the area and saw several horses tied up in the shade behind Sheffler's Saloon. "How about borrowing a couple of those over there?"

Earp looked in the same direction, smiled, and said, "What's that old sailor's saying about any port in a storm? I think we ought to borrow a couple of horses, too. I don't know that we'll be able to get close enough to those fanatics in Patton's automobile."

Earp and Mitchell helped themselves to two mounts and rode off almost unnoticed by anyone. Only the guard and his superior saw them ride away.

"We'd better tell the colonel about this," said the senior official, "as soon as he finishes speaking."

Earp considered the situation as they galloped toward the area where he was certain Friedkin and Beal were waiting to blow up Roosevelt's train.

Except for a few palo verde trees in the washes, the desert offered no protective foliage. The only possible hiding places were the ravines themselves and a few rocky outcroppings. This was good and bad. It would make finding Friedkin and Beal easy enough, but it would also make it difficult to come on them in surprise. Since the railroad had to circle around the foothills to get to Granite Pass but the road didn't, approaching from higher ground seemed to be the logical thing to do.

Earp and Mitchell followed the road to the low hills at the approach to Granite Pass, then they turned off the highway and rode up the first ridge. Reaching the crest, they halted and surveyed the slope slanting toward the railroad but saw nothing suspicious. They moved on to the next hill and scanned the area below.

"See that clump of trees down there?" asked Earp. "That wash is pretty deep down there, and there's a bridge farther down. Let's dismount here and go down for a look-see. You take the left ridge, and I'll take the right, and we'll come up on both sides. If they're down there, maybe we can get the drop on them. Keep to the outside of the ridge and try to be as quiet as you can. If they do see us first, we can drop below the ridge for cover. Okay?"

"You would have made a good general, Mr. Earp," said Mitchell. "You've got a good grasp of military tactics."

"That's funny. I always thought it was called plain old common sense."

Red-faced, Mitchell said, "I never thought of it that way, but I guess you're right."

They climbed down from the horses, made sure they tied the reins to the nearest mesquite bush, then pulled the rifles from their saddle cases. Earp had a Winchester .44, and Mitchell had a later model, the Winchester .44-40. They checked to make certain the guns were loaded.

"Let's go," said Earp.

Slowly, they worked their way down the hill toward the trees. Mitchell, being younger and a little more eager for a fight, was taking three steps for every two Earp took. In seconds, he was yards ahead. He was a little more than halfway down when he saw Friedkin and Beal crouching under the trees, a dynamite plunger between them.

In the distance, the whistle of Roosevelt's train announced its departure from Salome. It would be only a matter of eight or nine minutes before the train would be crossing the bridge at the base of the hill.

Mitchell looked over at Earp and signaled him with a wave of a hand and the pointing of a finger. Earp responded in a similar manner, indicating to Mitchell that he should move out of sight farther down the outside of the ridge. Mitchell understood and followed orders.

In another minute, Mitchell was almost parallel to the clump of palo verdes. He creeped up to the crest of the ridge and peeked over it to see Beal and Friedkin waiting patiently for their prey. There was no reason to hesitate, so he jumped up and trained the Winchester on them.

"Put your hands up!" shouted Mitchell.

Beal and Friedkin turned and faced him, both totally surprised.

"And move away from that plunger!"

Earp heard Mitchell shout, so he moved into position to cover the captain. He still couldn't see Beal and Friedkin, but he could see Charlotte Simpson.

Charlotte was sitting on a blanket in the middle of a trio of trees; one of them had hidden her from Mitchell's and Earp's views when they were coming down the hill and another was now shielding her from Mitchell's sight. Slowly and quietly, she reached for a rifle that lay beside her.

Earp raised his Winchester and fired a warning shot over her head. She turned toward him, her mouth wide open in frightened surprise.

"Just let that rifle be, Miss Simpson," said Earp. "There won't be anyone getting killed today."

THIRTY

Since Salome had no jail and because Siringo requested it, Sheriff Farnsworth had the prisoners taken to Harqua Hala.

Patton stayed on in Harqua Hala at Colonel Hardesty's order. The Army wanted Ardmore Simpson, and Patton was told to put forth their claim on him.

Earp and Siringo still had a murder case to solve. With Jake Poole's help they conducted a few searches. Then, satisfied that they had all the facts necessary to the solution, they gathered all seven of their suspects in the jailhouse.

Farnsworth sat at the deputy's desk almost like a judge at a trial. Present were Earp, Siringo, and Patton; the seven suspects: Mamie Sattin, Ardmore Simpson, Charlotte Simpson, Big George Kramer, Horace Beal, Hans Friedkin, and Jake Poole; and Lester T. Higgins, who was there at Earp's request. Farnsworth stared at each face, then fixed his gaze on Earp.

"All right, Wyatt," said Farnsworth, "which one of them killed Walt?"

"Charlie and I have a difference of opinion on that, Clyde," said Earp. "So we thought we'd let you decide which one of us is right."

"Is that right?" said Farnsworth. "You mean to tell me you still don't know for sure which one of those varmints killed Walt?"

Siringo lowered his head and said, "Well, each one of us has a pretty good case, but we're both missing one critical piece of evidence. So we thought you should listen to what we've come up with and maybe you could put in the last piece for one of us."

Farnsworth shook his head in disbelief. "You two are really something else. You come here to find a killer, but instead of that, you stop a train holdup, then foil a plot to kill Roosevelt. I don't believe this, but let's get on with it. Who's first?"

"Wyatt, be my guest," said Siringo.

"Thank you, Charlie," said Earp. "Clyde, I'm of the opinion that Big George Kramer is the killer."

"I told you before," growled Kramer, "I didn't kill anyone."

"Clyde, I guess you know Mr. Higgins here," said Earp.

"Undertaker, right?"

"That's me, Sheriff," said Higgins.

"Well, Mr. Higgins doesn't miss too much around this town," said Earp. "He happened to be awake the night Walt was killed, and he just happened to see Big George out and about that night. Isn't that right, Mr. Higgins?"

"You bet, Wyatt. I couldn't sleep that night, so I went for a walk. I was walking by the alley between the jail here and the newspaper office when I saw Kramer leaving by way of Beal's back door. I didn't pay no attention to it because I've seen him leave there late at night on several occasions. Then I walked around the newspaper office and was passing the mining company office when I heard the first shot. I wasn't sure where it came from, but something made me head back toward the alley. I cut between the mining company office and the newspaper. That's when I saw Big George again. He was running through the livery stable corral. Before I could think too much about it, there was folks all over the place and someone found poor Walt's body."

"Why didn't you tell me this when I was here questioning everyone?" asked Farnsworth.

"First off," said Higgins, "you didn't ask me. Second, I couldn't say for sure that Big George did it, and I ain't one to point no fingers until I'm one hundred percent positive of what I know."

"Is that right?" said Farnsworth.

"Then," said Earp, "Mamie here told me that Big George was late getting back to the saloon when Walt's body was brought in. Finally, Big George has a shotgun." Earp walked over to a corner and picked up the weapon that was leaning against the wall. "This is it, Clyde. I had Jake go through Big George's room, and he found these shells there." Earp produced two empty double-ought shotgun shells from his coat pocket. "This all adds up to Big George being Walt's killer. Leastwise, it does to me."

"I told you," said Kramer, "I didn't do it. The old man is right. I did come out of Beal's place just before the shooting, and I did run through the corral after I heard the shots. But that was because I thought someone was shooting at me. I tell you, I didn't do it."

"Then who did?" asked Farnsworth.

"It was Friedkin," said Kramer.

"Me? I didn't kill anyone. Simpson had his hired gun do it."

"That's a lie!" snapped Simpson. "I had no reason to have Walt killed."

"Didn't you?" said Beal. "Walt found out about your little mining operation over to Granite Pass, didn't he? Wasn't that reason enough to kill him?"

"Yeah," said Farnsworth. "What about that?"

"Okay, so he found out," said Simpson. "So what?"

"So you killed him to keep him from telling everyone about it," said Beal.

"I tell you—"

"Hold on, Simpson," said Farnsworth. "You keep quiet for a minute. I want to know why Big George thinks Friedkin did it."

"He was at that meeting, too," said Kramer. "He left just before I did. He hated Walt and wanted to kill him because Walt was his real father. All he had to do was wait in Mrs. Gianelli's backyard for Walt to come out of the jail and make his rounds. Then after he shot him, all he had to do was run into the house."

"No good," said Earp. "Mamie would have seen him from her window if he'd been hiding in Mrs. Gianelli's backyard. Did you see him there, Mamie?"

"I didn't see anyone," said Mamie.

"Besides," said Earp, "Friedkin doesn't own a shotgun. Or at least Jake couldn't find one when he searched his room at Mrs. Gianelli's."

"But Simpson owns one," said Friedkin.

"So do a lot of people in town," said Simpson. "What does that prove?"

"It proves a lot," said Siringo. "If you don't mind, Clyde, this is getting us no place. Wyatt's had his turn. I'd like to take mine now."

"Go ahead, Charlie," said Farnsworth. "Let's hear it."

"First off," said Siringo, "I hope you don't take offense at this, Wyatt, but you haven't gone about this thing very scientifically. There's a real science to detective work, and although I'm no master at it, I do my best to get facts instead of working with assumptions. You understand, don't you, Wyatt?"

Earp smiled and said, "No offense taken, Charlie. That's why I asked you in on this in the first place."

"Thank you, Wyatt," said Siringo. "Okay, I'll go on. First let's look at the facts. Walt was killed with a shotgun. We know that Big George owns a shotgun and he had double-ought shells. We also know Simpson owns a shotgun. Jake here has a shotgun right in this office. Even Mr. Beal owns a shotgun, don't you, Mr. Beal?"

"Yes, but I didn't kill anyone with it."

"We'll see about that," said Siringo. "But let me go on first. Now the question is motive. Why would any of these people want to kill Walt Phillips?" He made a sweeping motion with his hand. "Everyone here except Mr. Higgins had a reason to kill Walt. Even you, Mamie, as you already indicated to Wyatt. We won't go into details, but Walt was indirectly responsible for Mamie being in her current position. Mr. Friedkin, you knew Walt was your natural father, but do you know who your mother is?"

Friedkin looked at Siringo defiantly and said, "She was a great lady."

"Knowing her personally," said Siringo, looking at Mamie, "I have to agree. Mamie, Wyatt and I meant to talk to you about this, but the opportunity escaped us. So I hope you'll forgive me for this shock. Mamie, I would like you to meet your son." He waved toward Friedkin.

Mamie was aghast, as was almost everyone except Earp and Siringo.

Before anyone could interrupt, Siringo went on with his monologue. "And you, Mr. Friedkin, hated Walt and wanted him dead because he was your natural father and had deserted your mother, who was forced to give you up for adoption. Isn't that right?"

Friedkin didn't answer Siringo. Instead, he looked at Mamie and softly said, "You are my mother?"

Mamie's eyes were filled with tears. "I am if your real mother's name was May Belle Weaver."

Friedkin moved across the room slowly and knelt at Mamie's feet. Glassy-eyed, he said, "It was."

Leave it to the hardened lawman to interrupt the reunion. Farnsworth cleared his throat and said, "There'll be time for that later. Get on with it, Charlie."

"Yes, of course," said Siringo. "Well, we already know why Simpson wanted Walt dead, as much as he may deny it. But what about these other people, including you, Jake? Why would any of them want Walt dead? Jake wanted Walt's job, that's for sure. But Jake wouldn't kill Walt for it. What about Beal and Kramer? They were plotting to kill Roosevelt, and maybe Walt discovered their plot. If so, they would want Walt out of the way. But we don't know that Walt ever learned about their plot. And now we come to you, Miss Simpson. For the life of me, I can't think of why you would want to kill Walt. Unless, of course, you— No, I'm getting ahead of myself."

"Let's go back to the facts," said Siringo, continuing. "Specifically, the shotgun. It was a very unusual shotgun that killed Walt." He picked up Kramer's gun and held it by the stock, barrels down. "Most shotguns have convex butts like this one. The one that killed Walt had a stock like a rifle, one where the butt curves inward."

"How do you know that?" asked Farnsworth.

"Before I answer that, Clyde," said Siringo, "let me tell you what Mamie told Wyatt and me. She said that she could see the shotgun blast from her window but she couldn't see the killer. I checked out her story by examining the area where Walt was killed. I found two marks in the fence gate that appear to have been made by a rifle butt. Jake, bring me Simpson's shotgun."

Poole complied.

"If you'll notice," said Siringo, holding the firearm in the same manner as he had held Kramer's weapon, "this gun has a concave butt like a rifle. And if you'll also notice, this piece has a metal plate over the butt with Simpson's name in raised letters. This plate matches the marks in Mrs. Gianelli's fence gate perfectly, but that isn't what led me to my conclusion as to who the killer is.

"The puzzling part of the marks in the fence gate was their height from the ground," said Siringo. "They were too low to have been made by a man, and besides, a man wouldn't have needed to use the gate to hold the gun steady. A woman would have, though." He turned to Charlotte Simpson. "That's what made me suspect you, Miss Simpson."

"Wait a minute, you old fool!" snapped Charlotte. "I didn't kill him."

Siringo ignored her protest and continued. "Then when Wyatt and Captain Mitchell captured these anarchists, Miss Simpson had a rifle with her. A Winchester . . . .30-30. When Wyatt said she had a rifle, I had hoped it was a .32 Special, because that was the weapon used by the bushwhacker who fired at George and me the other day. Then Jake and I searched through Ben Kilpatrick's belongings, and we found a .32 Special rifle. So I was back to wondering if Miss Simpson was guilty or not."

"I told you—"

Siringo held up a hand to stop her, then said, "As I was saying before, I couldn't for the life of me figure out why Miss Simpson would want to kill Walt. Then I recalled something Mamie told us early on. Mamie, would you mind recalling the night of Walt's murder once more for us?"

"No, not at all," said Mamie. "What about it?"

"Earlier in the evening," said Siringo, "you said there was a disturbance upstairs at the Dutchman's. Is that correct?"

"That's right," said Mamie. "Friedkin . . . I mean, Hans. Hans came up quite drunk and—"

"Thank you, Mamie. That's all I wanted to hear. Like I said before, I thought the marks in the gate were made by the shotgun butt because a woman was holding the gun. Then I thought that just maybe they weren't made by a woman holding the gun but that they were made because the man holding the gun was so drunk he couldn't hold the shotgun properly."

"But I didn't do it," said Friedkin. "I spent the night in jail."

"That's right," said Poole. "I can vouch for that."

"Mamie," said Siringo, "would you go on about that night?"

"Well, like I was saying, Hans came up drunk and broke in on Simpson and one of my girls. They got into it pretty good until Big George came up and stopped it. Then Walt and Jake came up, and Walt took Hans off to jail."

"What happened to Simpson?" asked Siringo.

"I took him home," said Poole.

"Why?" asked Siringo.

"Because he was so drunk he couldn't hardly stand up," said Poole.

"That's right," said Mamie. "He was drunk that night."

"So drunk," said Siringo, "that he got up the nerve to kill Walt Phillips. Isn't that right, Simpson?"

"That's preposterous!" snapped Simpson. "I was home in bed, sleeping it off."

"No, Father, you weren't," said the daughter.

"Charlotte, what are you saying?" stammered the suddenly nervous father.

"I had just gotten home from our meeting at the newspaper that night," said Charlotte, "and you weren't home."

"Will you testify to that, Miss Simpson?" asked Farnsworth.

"Charlotte, I'm your father," said Simpson, his voice pleading with his daughter.

Charlotte looked intensely at Simpson, but there was no love in her eyes for him. "Yes, I will testify."

About the Author

Larry Names's writing career began at age eleven when his first article was published in the Mt. Pleasant (Michigan) *Daily Times-News*. As a teenager he was a prep sports reporter for the Riverside (California) *Press-Enterprise*. An essay on John F. Kennedy's assassination drew national attention when it was picked up and published in major newspapers across the nation.

Names continued his career in journalism by becoming a stringer, then sports editor for *The Waushara Argus* (Wisconsin), then became sports editor for the Broken Arrow *Daily Ledger* (Oklahoma). In 1979 he was named managing editor of the Las Vegas *Voice* (Nevada).

While working for the Phoenix *Gazette* (Arizona) in 1974, Names began his first novel, *The Legend of Eagle Claw* (Independence Press, 1980). He is the author of seven other books:

Twice Dead (Leisure Books, 1978)

The Shaman's Secret (Doubleday, 1979)

Bose (Doubleday, 1980)

The Pro Writer (Laranmark, 1981)

Boomtown (Doubleday, 1982)

The History of the Green Bay Packers—Book I (Angel Press of WI, 1987)

The History of the Chicago Cubs—Book I (Angel Press of WI, 1987)

Larry Names was born in Mishawaka, Indiana, on February 27, 1947, to Charles and Lois Names. Names, his wife Peggy, and their six-year-old son, Tory, live in an old farmhouse in rural Neshkoro (Wisconsin), which they are just beginning to renovate. He also has four children (Sigrid, Paul, Kristin, and Sonje) from a previous marriage.